PONY 🐎 CLUB, SECRETS

Liberty and the Dream Ride

The Pony Club Secrets series:

Also available in the series:

Issie and the Christmas Pony

(Christmas special)

Final book in the series coming soon . . .

PONY CLUB SECRETS

Liberty and the Dream Ride

STACY GREGG

HarperCollins *Children's Books*

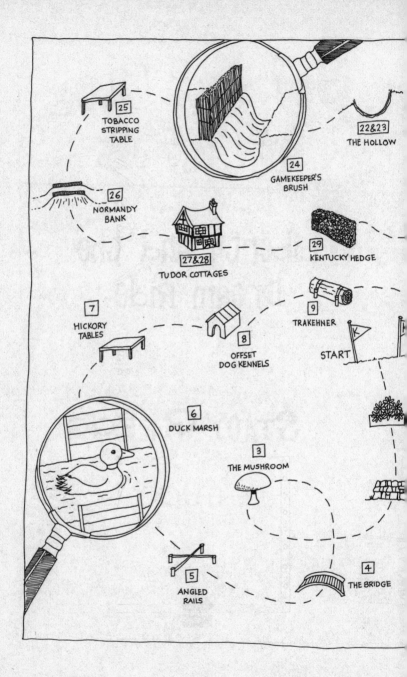

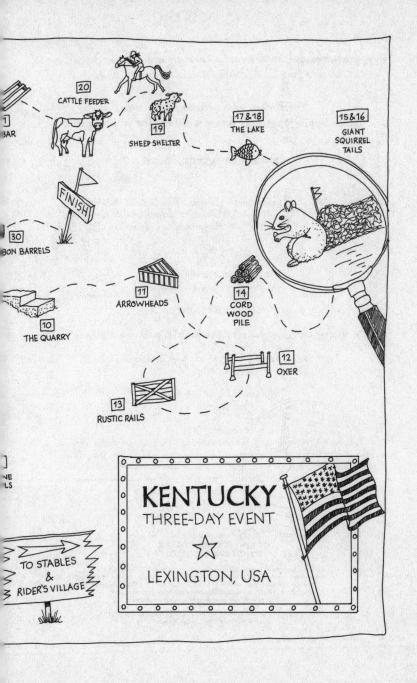

Congratulations and thanks to India Lambeth who won our competition to "name a pony". India's horse Avatar appears in this book.

**For Parker, who arrived just in time.
Here's hoping that your future will be filled with ponies…**

www.stacygregg.co.uk

First published in Great Britain by HarperCollins *Children's Books* in 2011
HarperCollins *Children's Books* is a division of HarperCollins*Publishers* Ltd,
77-85 Fulham Palace Road, Hammersmith, London, W6 8JB.

1

Text copyright © Stacy Gregg 2011
Illustrations © Fiona Land 2011

ISBN 978-0-00-729931-7

Stacy Gregg asserts the moral right to be identified as the author of the work.

Typeset in AGaramond by Palimpsest Book Production Limited,
Falkirk, Stirlingshire

Printed and bound in England by
Clays Ltd, St Ives plc

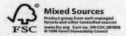

Chapter 1

The horses inside the belly of the 747 cargo plane were restless. For eleven long hours they had been cooped up in their tiny stalls, unable to move or do anything more than nibble at their hay nets. Now, at last, they were almost there. Dawn was breaking across the skies above Los Angeles and very soon the plane would be landing and the horses would be craned down on to the tarmac in their shipping stalls, ready to be moved on to their final destinations.

There were three horses in the transporter stalls on this flight. In the first was a sleek mahogany bay Thoroughbred, bound for the racetracks of Flushing Meadows and Belmont. Too nervous to eat, the bay horse hadn't touched his hay net for the entire journey. He was anxiously moving about in his tiny stall, disturbed by the whine of the plane engines and the strange smells and sounds all around him, an atmosphere so different to his serene life in the stables back home in England.

Beside the Thoroughbred, standing in the next stall, was a chestnut stallion. He was even bigger than the bay, standing at seventeen hands. He was solidly built, a heavy-set Oldenburg with a muscular physique that could have been carved from granite. The sire of countless colts and fillies, this Oldenburg stallion possessed a bloodline that was valuable beyond measure. Like the Thoroughbred, he had been restless throughout the flight, fretting and snorting at every sudden bump and jolt of turbulence.

The third horse onboard the plane looked positively tiny by comparison. He was a mere pony – standing only fourteen-two hands high. Unlike the Thoroughbred and the Oldenburg, who clearly had noble blood in their veins, this pony was a ragamuffin. His stocky conformation and coarse chestnut and white skewbald coat betrayed his lack of breeding. He had spent most of his life sleeping rough without so much as a rug, even in winter. He had never been pampered and he certainly wasn't accustomed to being on fancy jet planes. And yet, of all the three horses, he was the one that had coped the best with this epic journey. He had settled immediately in his stall and during the course of the trip he'd eaten his way through a miraculous eight netfuls of hay and kept the two grooms assigned to his care constantly on their feet with his antics and demands.

"He's a real comedian," the groom with bushy eyebrows said as he offered the skewbald water from the bucket he was holding. He stood and watched the gelding make a fuss, snorting and blowing theatrically as he drank.

"Did you see the way he swiped my sandwich out of my hand this morning?" the other groom, a sandy-haired man replied. "Man, he is one cheeky pony! I'm really gonna miss the little fella."

"Well, I ain't gonna miss him!" The groom with the bushy eyebrows glared at the skewbald. "He pick-pocketed my cellphone when I was doing up his halter and he bit the aerial off before I could get it back again!"

"What breed do you suppose he is, anyway?" The

sandy-haired groom, whose name was Clement, leant up against his stall and stared at the skewbald. "He don't look like no purebred I've ever seen."

The bushy-browed groom was called Harrison. He eyed the skewbald warily before stepping forward to lift the clipboard down off the wall to examine the pony's paperwork. "It says here he's a Blackthorn Pony," he replied. "Now what in the blue blazes is a Blackthorn Pony?"

"I've heard about them," Clement said. "They're from New Zealand, a wild breed from the hill country near Gisborne. They're small, just like this little guy here, but they're bred to jump."

"Well this one must jump pretty darn high," Harrison said, "because it says here that he's travelling to Lexington for the Kentucky Three-Day Event."

"You're kidding me!" Clement said. "That's a Four-Star competition! The best eventing horses in the world are going to be competing at Kentucky. That's no place for a little guy like this."

The bushy-browed man shrugged. "I ain't arguing with you, Clement, but that's what it says on the forms."

Clement gazed at the skewbald and shook his head

in disbelief. "What kind of a crazy man takes a pony like this to a competition like that?"

Harrison examined the skewbald's paperwork. "Not a man," he said, "a girl."

He peered at the papers. "This pony's owned by some teenager and she's requested fast-tracking through quarantine because she's planning to ride him in a week's time in the Four-Star."

"So you're telling me that a teenage girl is riding him at Kentucky?" Clement said. "All right then, what's the name?"

"It says here the pony is called Comet."

"No, no," Clement shook his head. "Not the pony's name! I mean the girl! What's the girl's name?"

"Oh, right." Harrison shuffled through the papers once again. "Here it is!" he said at last. "The rider's name is Brown... Isadora Brown."

Isadora Brown stood on the tarmac at Los Angeles Airport, shielding her eyes with her hands as she peered into the sky.

"I hope he's OK, Tom," she said to the tall man with brown curly hair standing beside her. "You know what Comet's like. He's not used to standing still for more than a minute. He's probably tried to jump out of the shipping stall by now. Eleven whole hours in a plane is going to drive him insane…"

"Issie, relax!" Tom Avery said. "He'll be fine. Have you ever known Comet to be fazed by anything?"

"As long as there's food he'll be happy," Stella agreed. "That pony is ruled by his stomach!" She looked over at Avery. "Do you suppose the horses get to choose what they eat on the plane?"

Avery frowned. "What are you talking about, Stella?"

"You know, do they get a menu?" Stella said. "Can they choose, like, the vegetarian option?"

"Stella, they don't get served dinner on a tray. All they get is hay," Avery said. "And do I really have to make the obvious point that all horses are vegetarians?"

The bubbly red-head was about to open her mouth to speak again before Avery added, "And before you ask an even stupider question, the answer is no, there are no in-flight movies for the horses. It's a cargo plane, for Pete's sake!"

"Poor ponies," Stella said, "how boring for them."

"Hey!" Issie pointed at a plane taxiing towards them. "Look! That must be him!"

The plane with three distinctive red cubes painted on the tail eased to a stop beside the cargo hangar. Issie wanted more than anything to race out across the tarmac and greet her horse, but she was caged behind the wire fence surrounding the quarantine area.

Issie groaned. "This is awful, being so close, but not being able get to him!"

"It's only another forty-eight hours," Avery said, "just until he clears quarantine. We'll fill in the paperwork today and then in two days we can claim him from the stables…"

Issie was only half listening. She was staring at the crates being forklifted from the 747 on to the tarmac. She'd watched a bay horse and a chestnut being loaded out and now at last she caught sight of a familiar face with chestnut and white patches sticking up over the top of the high walls of the shipping crate. There he was, with his usual cheeky expression, his eyes bright and curious as he checked out his new surroundings.

"Comet! Over here!" Issie shouted, but her voice was drowned out by the noise of the jet engines. "Comet!" she tried again and this time the pony heard her. His ears pricked forward and he turned his face in her direction and gave a vigorous whinny as if to say "Hey! Here I am! Get me out of here!"

Comet's eyes were glittering with excitement, his nostrils wide. He gave another wild whinny and Issie shouted back to him. "Only two more days! I'll see you soon!" She pressed her face to the wire mesh as the forklift picked up Comet's crate once more and ferried the shipping stall away towards the hangar at the far end of the runway.

Issie watched him go, the wind from the jet engines whipping her long dark hair against her cheeks. She felt Avery's hand on her shoulder. "They'll take good care of him," her trainer reassured her. "These international air-transit grooms are experts in equine care, they know exactly what to do. Comet will have lost as much as twenty kilos from dehydration on that flight. He'll need to drink and eat lots to get over his journey. By the time we get him on Thursday he'll be fit and ready to leave for Lexington."

"Until then," Stella said, "I say we go sightseeing. I've got a map of LA with all the celebrity mansions marked on it. We should go down Hollywood Boulevard and check out the Walk of Fame…"

She noticed Avery glaring at her. "What?"

"Stella," Avery said, "we're not here on holiday. Kentucky is Issie's first Four-Star event and as her groom you have work to do. Once Comet is free from quarantine we'll be on the road to Lexington and we need to be prepared. In just nine days the competition gets underway."

"Umm, the thing is, Tom…" Issie hesitated, "we were thinking maybe we could spend a day at Disneyland and—"

"Disneyland! What the…?" Avery sputtered in disbelief. "Isadora! You're seventeen years old. This isn't some pony club rally we're about to face – this is serious stuff, and you want to take off on a tour of The Mickey Mouse Club? Have you lost sight of how important this is?"

"No," Issie replied quietly, "of course not."

She didn't need reminding. She knew how much was riding on her success at Lexington. This was the culmination of everything she had worked so hard for over the past two years, ever since she had returned from Spain with Nightstorm to Chevalier Point.

When Issie had brought Nightstorm home to New Zealand she had immediately set about schooling him as an eventer, with Avery as her trainer. The big bay stallion had been a quick learner and by the end of the first season she was riding both Comet and Nightstorm on the eventing circuit, attending horse trials around the country, and getting as many One and Two-Star competitions under her belt as she possibly could.

Then, at the end of last year, just as Issie was about to sit her GCSE exams, Avery had come to her with a momentous offer. "The past year has gone really well," he told her, "but if you really want to turn professional then we need to base ourselves where the action is." Avery looked serious. "I think we should move to England."

Even though she hated the idea of leaving Chevalier Point behind, Issie knew that it made sense. Most of the top-flight Three-Star events were held in the UK and Europe and she needed to gain international experience riding the big cross-country courses if she wanted to progress.

So, in the final weeks of the school year, while Issie was sitting her exams, Avery began the complex process of moving the team to the UK. He handed over the management of Dulmoth Park and Winterflood Farm to his head groom, Verity. Dulmoth Park's owner Cassandra Steele had been sorry to lose Avery and Issie, but when it was explained to her that Verity would train up the young eventers in New Zealand and then send them on to England for Issie to ride on the international circuit, Cassandra gave the team her wholehearted support.

Avery's departure also caused a stir at the Chevalier Point Pony Club as it meant that the coveted position of head instructor now became vacant. There were lots of applicants, but in the end it was one of Issie's best friends, Kate Knight, who was appointed as his successor. Kate had always been brilliant at teaching young riders and her new role would fit in perfectly with her studies at the vet school she would soon be attending.

Issie had wanted to move to the UK with Avery immediately, but her mum insisted that she sit her

GCSEs before she went. And so Avery and his wife, the famed dressage trainer Francoise D'Arth, had gone on ahead to England without her. Issie was thrilled when they emailed back to say that they had found the perfect place to set up their new UK base – a small stables called Laurel Farm, deep in the heart of rural Wiltshire.

With a dozen loose boxes, a manege and twenty acres of meadowland bordered by forest that was ideal for hacking, Laurel Farm was one of the prettiest stables in England. Francoise D'Arth was responsible for the day-to-day running of this new venture, exercising the horses as well as continuing to provide tuition as Issie's dressage trainer. Nightstorm and Comet made the flight from New Zealand to England before Issie. They would now live at Laurel Farm, along with half a dozen other young up-and-coming eventers that Francoise was schooling up for the future.

Staying back at school proved worthwhile when Issie aced her exams, and just a week after getting her results she was boarding a plane to England, along with Stella Tarrant, her best friend, who had gladly agreed to come with her to be Laurel Farm's head groom.

Avery wasted no time and as soon as they arrived, the two girls were thrust into the demanding life of the European eventing circuit. Over the next year they were on the road with Avery, driving their horse lorry all around Europe to competitions on such a constant basis that Issie never bothered to unpack her suitcase. It was like being a pop star on tour – always in a different city, losing track of the time zones and the language that she was supposed to be speaking!

Being on the road was exhausting, but it paid off. By the end of the season Issie had risen up the professional rankings and was in the top ten of the prestigious international young rider table. The pinnacle of her achievement was an astonishing win against some legendary competition at the famous Bramham Park Three-Star where she took out first place with a double clear on the cross-country and the showjumping phases.

Winning was great – but the prize money at Bramham had barely covered their running costs. Eventing was a very expensive sport and all the really big superstars like Piggy French and William Fox-Pitt survived on sponsorship money to support their stables.

For an up-and-coming rider like Issie there was no chance of getting a sponsor to pay the bills. Laurel Farm was beginning to build up a string of promising horses, but they had absolutely zero cash. As Avery put it, they were "on the boniest, bony bones of their bottoms".

One night around the kitchen table, Avery, Francoise, Issie and Stella made the sad decision to sell Amaretto, one of Laurel Farm's most promising young eventing horses, to raise enough funds for Issie, Avery, Stella and Comet to travel to the Kentucky Four-Star.

Issie had felt awful about parting with one of their best horses, but they had no choice. She knew that this was the hard truth all competitive riders faced – selling off their best horses just to stay in the game. And if Issie couldn't finish in the top ten rankings in Kentucky and claim some of the prize money, then things would only get worse. Next time she would be forced to choose one of her advanced eventers, and either Comet or Nightstorm could be up for sale when she got home.

Issie didn't even want to think about it! Instead she was pinning her hopes on recouping prize money in Kentucky. The winner of the three-day event would receive an amazing $100,000! The fate of Issie's horses, and the future of Laurel Farm, was riding on her success in Kentucky. Avery was right – things had changed. This was the big league – they weren't kids any more. And this was no trip to Disneyland.

Chapter 2

Issie stood anxiously waiting at the front desk while the quarantine agent worked his way slowly and meticulously through the pages of Comet's paperwork.

"Has he been behaving himself?" she asked the quarantine agent nervously. "I'm sorry if he's been any trouble. Comet's not naughty exactly, but he doesn't like loose boxes, and he gets bored. One time he tried to roll in his box and then he got his head stuck in a feed bucket and couldn't get it off!"

Issie grinned, but the quarantine agent appeared unmoved. He looked up briefly from his paperwork, frowned and then typed something else into the computer on his desk before returning to the stack of papers. Issie looked at her watch. How much longer was this going to take? She'd been at the desk for nearly an hour! Finally, the official reached for the large rubber stamp on his desk and brought it down with a thump on top of Comet's forms.

"OK. You've been approved. It's all in order," he told Issie gruffly, pushing the papers back across the desk towards her. "Take these with you and present them at the front gate. They'll let you enter the compound and pick up your horse."

The guard at the stable block was no friendlier. "What's the name of the horse that you're collecting?" he asked without looking up as he flicked through the papers.

"Comet," Issie said.

As Issie's voice echoed down the corridor of the stables, there was a sudden sound of hooves stamping on the straw from inside one of the loose boxes. A moment later a skewbald face appeared over one of the Dutch doors and Comet began whinnying and flicking his head up and down.

"Your horse?" the guard asked with a raised eyebrow.
"Uh-huh." Issie beamed.

"You can go and collect him out of the loose box if you want," the guard said.

Issie didn't need to be told twice – she raced down the corridor to greet her pony.

"Hey, boy." She patted Comet's broad white stripe. "How are you? Have they been treating you OK in here? Have you made friends with the other horses?"

Comet was nickering vigorously, telling Issie all about his epic plane journey and the days of boredom in quarantine.

Issie listened and nodded sympathetically. "I know, I've missed you too, but it's OK now, we're here to take you with us. We're going to Kentucky."

She clipped the lead shank to the pony's halter and led him out of his stall. She could hear the other horses in their stalls whinnying their goodbyes as she led the skewbald down the corridor of the stable block. Massive electronic gates swung open to let them out into the bright sunshine of the quarantine yard where Avery and Stella were waiting with the rental horse float hitched up to the back of their Jeep.

"Ohmygod, we've been waiting hours!" Stella said as

she helped lower the ramp of the horse float so they could load him onboard.

"Let's get moving," Avery told them. "We want to be on the freeway and out of Los Angeles before the traffic gets heavy."

The skewbald was looking around the yard, his ears pricked forward. When he saw the rickety horse float that Avery was towing behind the Jeep, however, his ears went back. He refused to step up the ramp and in the end Avery had to place a lunge rope around his rump to urge him onboard.

"Poor Comet," Stella said. "I'm not surprised he doesn't want to get on – look at the state of it!"

The horse float they'd hired was an ancient contraption. Issie had been quietly horrified when they picked it up from the rental yards yesterday and she saw the peeling blue paint flaking off the framework exposing the rust underneath. There was black lettering around the front of the float that must once have said *Horse Star*, but a couple of the letters had rusted away so that the sign read *Hose tar*.

"What's a 'hose tar'?" Stella had wrinkled her nose up.

"Umm… Is this thing actually roadworthy?" Issie had asked nervously.

Avery had clambered about underneath the chassis and pronounced the horse box perfectly sound. "It's not pretty, but it will get us to Kentucky."

Now, with Comet finally loaded onboard, they pulled out on to the Los Angeles freeway, and listened as their satnav gave Avery directions through the complicated spaghetti junctions of the city, until finally they were on the open roads of Route 40, heading towards Kentucky.

By midday the landscape had changed. The houses had disappeared and been replaced by desert. The view out the car windows was like watching a cowboy movie, nothing but dust and cacti as far as the eye could see.

"You couldn't keep a horse here," Stella observed. "This is terrible grazing!"

She gazed out the window wistfully. "I can't wait to get to Kentucky to see the *blue* grass."

"What?" Avery looked at her like she was mad. "Stella, Lexington, Kentucky is called 'bluegrass country', but it's a nickname – it doesn't mean they really have blue grass."

"Well what colour is it then?" Stella said.

"It's green, Stella," Avery rolled his eyes. "Just like ordinary grass."

"Well that is majorly disappointing!" Stella flopped back in her seat. "I thought it would be like Smurf-land or something."

Issie looked at her watch. "What time is it in New Zealand?" she asked Avery.

"About five p.m.," Avery said. "You can call your mother when we stop for lunch if you like."

Issie looked around at the alien landscape of the Mojave Desert and felt a sudden pang of homesickness for her old life in Chevalier Point. She felt a bit weepy for a moment, but she knew she was just exhausted because of jetlag. She was still having trouble sleeping at night and kept waking up, sitting bolt upright in bed at three in the morning, unable to get back to sleep. And now, here they were in the middle of the day and she could hardly keep her eyes open.

"How come I have jetlag and Comet seems to be totally fine?" Issie asked Avery.

"Horses and humans react entirely differently to long-distance travel," Avery told her. "For horses, it takes several weeks for the jetlag to set in. Right now, Comet hasn't got jetlag at all. That's why we've brought him here on such a tight schedule right before the competition. The timing is crucial because we want him in peak condition and jetlag-free when we're in Kentucky."

Issie wished she was jetlag-free. She felt like an ocean tide was washing her in-and-out, in-and-out. Her brain was swimming in a warm pool, making it impossible to think clearly. As Avery drove on towards Flagstaff she was inexplicably gripped by a desperate urge to go to sleep, and so she succumbed.

It was probably the noise of the trucks whizzing by on the freeway that made her start dreaming. She had flashed back in time five years to that fateful day at Chevalier Point Pony Club. She could see it all so clearly, as if it was real – which of course it was, because this wasn't actually a dream. It was a memory, an event that had happened long ago, and that had haunted her ever since.

It was her very first gymkhana at Chevalier Point Pony Club and Issie and her pony Mystic had just left the show ring with a blue ribbon when chaos broke loose. Natasha Tucker had stamped out of the arena after losing the showjumping and in misguided fury she had viciously taken a swipe with her whip at her poor pony Goldrush. Issie watched in horror as the terrified Goldrush backed away and barged into Coco and Toby who were standing right beside her, tied to a horse truck. Natasha lost control of Goldrush completely and Coco and Toby both panicked and tore themselves free from the truck. Then all three horses bolted, heading straight for the pony-club gates.

As people began to run after the horses, trying to divert them before they reached the gate to the main road, Issie realised they'd never catch them in time on foot. But maybe she could reach them on Mystic.

The horses were out of the gates and had reached the road before Issie got to them. Cars were honking and swerving as she pulled Mystic around in front of Toby, and waved an arm at him, spooking the big bay, driving him back towards the pony club. The other two loose horses followed Toby's lead and scattered back off the road. Issie was just about to turn Mystic and follow them to safety when she heard the deep low boom of the truck horn. There was a sickening squeal of tyres as the truck driver tried to stop, and the intense smell of burning rubber as the truck went into a slide. To Issie, it seemed as if everything began to move in slow motion. She felt Mystic rear up beneath her to face the truck, like a stallion preparing to fight. As the grey pony went up on his hind legs he threw Issie back with such force that she flew clear out of the saddle.

She was falling, the tarmac racing up to meet her. She braced for the impact, but this time it never came. Instead, she was jolted out of her dream state by the sharp honk of a car horn and a man's voice shouting.

"Hey, buddy! You're on the wrong side of the road!"

She was suddenly wide awake. They were at a petrol station and Avery had just swerved to avoid another driver, honking vigorously and waving his fist as he went past them.

"Stupid Americans," Avery muttered under his breath, "It's not my fault you drive on the wrong side of the road. Why can't you drive on the left like everyone else?"

Then he caught sight of Issie's face.

"Are you all right, Issie?" he asked with genuine concern. "You look utterly exhausted. I'm sorry you got woken up."

"I'm fine," Issie said. "I guess I'm a bit jetlagged."

She was relieved that the honking had woken her up. At least she didn't have to relive the rest of that nightmare. After the fall on the road that day, Issie had been knocked out. She remembered the crack of her helmet on the tarmac, the taste of blood in her mouth and then everything had turned black.

When she woke up again, she was in a hospital bed with her mum sitting at her side holding her hand.

"Mum? Where is Mystic? Is Mystic OK?"

The look on her mother's face told her everything she needed to know even before she spoke. "Isadora, there was nothing anyone could have done... the truck... Mystic is dead."

Overwhelmed with grief at the loss of her beloved Mystic, Issie truly believed that she would never ride again – but then she didn't know what was to come, or that the bond she shared with Mystic would prove to be unbreakable.

The first time he returned, Issie didn't know how it could possibly be happening, and yet she instinctively knew somehow that the grey pony standing before her was real. Mystic had returned to her – not a ghost, but flesh and blood, and here to help her.

Ever since then Mystic had been her protector and her guardian, turning up out of the blue whenever Issie and her ponies really needed him.

Issie knew it wasn't just the jetlag that had brought on her dream. She'd had premonitions like this before. It was a sign that trouble was looming.

She didn't dare to fall asleep again. Instead, she stared out the car window, listening to the country music pouring out of the car stereo as they drove up mountain ranges through the dense conifer forests, and into the heartland of New Mexico.

It was almost seven and the sun was turning blood-red on the horizon when they finally reached their destination for the evening – a motel called The Hacienda on the outskirts of the township of Rio Rancho.

The motel buildings were old Spanish Mission plasterwork painted pale pink and there was a pink neon sign on the roof above the office that read: *Vacancy. Horses welcome.*

Stella stared at the sign with wide eyes. "I've never stayed at a horse motel before," she said. "Does Comet get his own bedroom or will he sleep with us?"

Avery looked at her. "Stella, they have loose boxes here for the horses."

"I was only joking," Stella grinned.

Avery backed the horse float up beside other floats parked in front of the stable block.

"I'll unload Comet," he told Issie. "You go in to the front desk and ask them for two rooms and a loose box for Comet. Oh, and get them to provide some hay too."

As she trudged across the motel forecourt, Issie realised that despite her nap in the car she was still exhausted. All she wanted to do was get those room keys, get Comet bedded down in his stall for the night and get some sleep.

At the reception desk, Issie waited patiently while an elderly couple checked in, and then it was her turn. She was about to step up to speak to the manager, when out of nowhere a boy slipped in front of her, barging in and taking her place.

"I'd like to book a room for the night, please..." the boy began.

Jetlagged and exhausted, Issie lost her cool. "Uhh, sorry, but I think I was next."

The boy turned around to look at her. He wasn't much older than Issie, and had short-cropped, ginger-blonde hair and wore dark blue jeans and a white T-shirt.

"Actually," he replied, in an English accent, "I was here first. You didn't notice me because I was just sitting down over there waiting."

"Sitting around isn't the same as being in the queue," Issie said. "I thought you English wrote the rule book on how to queue."

The boy gave a faint laugh. "There was no queue when I got here because *you* weren't here," he pointed out. "I was just waiting for my turn."

"Well it didn't look like you were queuing, that's all…"

"Ah, excuse me?" the motel manager spoke up. "Do either of you actually plan on checking in at any stage or is this going to go on forever?"

Issie sighed and gestured defeat with a tired wave of her hand. "You go ahead," she said to the boy.

"Thank you," he said and turned to the man at the desk. "Right! I'd like a room, please, and a loose box for my horse."

The man behind the counter handed him a key and pointed out the directions. "Park your horse truck over there with the others and you can put your horse in the last stall at the end of the stables."

The boy signed his name into the guest register and then gave Issie a grin. "*Now* it's your turn," he said.

Exhausted and fed up, Issie finally stepped up for her turn at the desk. "I'd like two rooms, please, and a loose box for my horse and hay for the evening."

The man shook his head. "Sorry, miss. No can do."

"What?" Issie was stunned. "What do you mean?"

"I've got the two rooms," the man continued, "but I haven't got any more horse stalls available."

The man behind the desk pointed out the doors to the boy in the white T-shirt outside in the forecourt.

"Your friend out there, he just took the last one."

Chapter 3

This was a nightmare! It was dark, they were exhausted, they had been travelling for twelve hours straight and there was nowhere else for them to go.

"I'm sorry," the motel manager said, "it's been crazy-busy today and I've got five horses checked in already – we've got no vacancies."

"Don't you have anything else at all?" Issie pleaded.

"Well," the man said, "that last stall I gave to the boy has a partition gate in it. You could always ask him if he's willing to share the loose box and get both your horses in there for the night."

Issie looked out of the doors of the motel reception.

The boy was by his truck on the forecourt, making a call on his mobile phone.

"I'll go and ask him," she told the motel manager. "I'll be right back."

The boy had pocketed his phone and was just about to climb back in his truck when Issie rushed over to him. "Hey!"

The boy looked up at her. She noticed at that moment that his hair was a really unusual colour, somewhere in between blond and copper, and that he had the coolest pale green eyes. "Yes?"

Issie took a deep breath and summoned up her last reserves of good humour and smiled at him. "I'm sorry about what happened in there."

"That's OK," the boy said, "don't worry about it."

"My name is Isadora, by the way," she said and stuck out her hand.

The boy took it and shook it. "I'm Marcus, Marcus Pearce."

He was about to climb into his truck, but Issie blocked his path. Marcus frowned at her. "Is there something else?"

"Ummm, yes," Issie said. "You see, the funny thing is, it turns out you got the last stall…"

"Is that so?" Marcus raised an eyebrow.

"… and I was just talking to the guy behind the desk and he suggested that your horse and my horse might, you know, share a stall for the night. There's a partition gate we can put in so they'd be kept separate and they'd be quite safe."

"Let me get this straight," Marcus said. "You want to share my stall?"

"Well," Issie couldn't help pointing out, "strictly speaking, if you hadn't pushed into the queue ahead of me then it would be my stall…"

Marcus shook his head in disbelief and began to get back in his truck again.

"Wait!" Issie said. "Please. My horse has nowhere else to sleep tonight and we've come all the way from Los Angeles and I'm jetlagged and I'm just really, really tired…"

Marcus raised a hand to stop her from continuing. "OK, OK. I guess I wouldn't be able to sleep if I knew your horse was stuck on the street for the night."

He smiled at her. "It looks like my mare has a new room-mate."

Avery and Stella already had Comet unloaded and waiting when Issie turned up with a total stranger in a sleek black horse truck.

"This is Marcus Pearce." Issie did the introductions. "They were short on stalls so he's offered to let his mare share with Comet."

Marcus grinned at the sight of the skewbald standing before him. "He's a cute little guy, isn't he?" he said. "Where are you taking him?"

"Lexington, Kentucky," Issie said. "We're competing in the Four-Star."

"You're kidding!"

"He's only a pony," Issie said, "but he's more impressive on the cross-country than he looks."

"I didn't mean it like that," Marcus said. "It's a coincidence, that's all. I'm riding at Kentucky too."

From inside Marcus's truck there came a whinny as if to confirm this, followed by the sound of hooves moving restlessly, thudding against the rubber-matting floor.

"I think my mare is tired of being cooped up," Marcus said. "I'd better unload her."

He lowered the truck ramp and the girls got a rear view of the mare's long silvery blonde tail and chocolate brown legs dressed in hock-high white sheepskin floating boots.

Marcus made gentle clucking noises at the mare to get her moving down the ramp, although she hardly needed much encouragement. After being on the road for so long she almost bounded off, her head held high and erect, nostrils wide with excitement as she sniffed the air and looked around.

Issie couldn't believe how pretty she was. The mare had a long silver-blonde mane that matched her lustrous tail, and her coat was a delicious cocoa colour with dapples in the chocolate on her rump and over her shoulders.

"She's unusual-looking, isn't she?" Marcus said as the girls stared at the mare. "She's a silver dapple."

Stella wrinkled her nose. "She looks more like chocolate to me."

"That's just what they call it," Marcus said. "A chocolate coat and a silver mane and tail. She's got three white socks underneath those floating boots too."

He ran a hand over the mare's neck. "My groom Annie is supposed to keep her mane short so that it's easy to plait for competitions, but she keeps letting it grow long because it's too pretty to pull."

Issie looked at the long forelock hanging down over the mare's eyes. "You should at least trim her forelock. I'm surprised she can even see the jumps from underneath all that hair!"

The mare seemed to know that everyone was talking about her. She moved about anxiously, her sheepskin-booted legs never staying still for more than a second. As she watched the mare strutting about, Issie put aside the mare's striking colour and examined her conformation with a cool, professional eye. The horse was a good size, about sixteen hands high, but lightly built with a lean frame and long legs that were perfect for travelling fast across country. Her shoulders had a perfect slope – the mark of a good mover – and she had exceptionally powerful hindquarters. It was the mare's face that Issie liked best, though. She had dainty white markings, a tiny white star beneath her silver-blonde forelock, and at the end of her muzzle there was a cute white snip as if she had dipped her nose into a pot of paint and then thought better of it. Her liquid brown eyes were wide set and intelligent.

"What's her name?" Issie asked.

"Valmont Liberty," said Marcus. "Valmont is the name of the stable that owns her – her name is Liberty."

As they'd been talking, Liberty had taken a good look around and now her eyes were locked on Comet. The skewbald gelding was being held by Stella just a few metres away and he was fidgeting at the end of the lead rope, keen to meet this newcomer.

"You wanna say hello, boy?" Stella led him forward so that he was close enough to greet the mare nose-to-nose.

"Watch it," Marcus warned. "She's a typical mare – she can be pretty grumpy around other horses."

As she touched muzzles with the gelding, Liberty's ears flattened back and she let out a guttural squeal, making it clear that she wasn't the slightest bit convinced about being friends.

But Comet wasn't to be deterred. He thrust his nose

out and nickered to the mare. Liberty had her ears hard back against her head, warning him off, but Comet kept his ears resolutely pricked forward, his eyes shining as he nickered to her again, trying to start a conversation. The mare stomped a hoof, her tail thrashed objectionably. She held her nose in the air, staring at this impertinent skewbald as if he were a commoner trying to make friends with a queen.

"She's not very friendly, is she?" Issie said.

"Oh, she's all right once you get to know her," Marcus insisted, giving the mare a firm pat on her glossy neck. He smiled at Issie. "Just like me, really."

The stalls for the horses at The Hacienda were a collection of covered yards, built in a U-shape around a dusty central courtyard behind the main building of the motel. Each of the covered yards was bordered by wooden railings and the floors of the stalls were covered in wood shavings for bedding. It was nice and clean, but it certainly wasn't fancy, Issie thought. Comet would be fine here – but a horse like Liberty was probably used to a life of luxury – a proper, elegant loose box.

"We should put the partition gate in between them tonight—" Marcus began to say as he led Liberty into the stalls, but before he could finish his sentence the mare intentionally swung her rump towards Comet and flung out a hind leg, taking a swift and vicious kick at the gelding, which thankfully missed its target. "I can't risk Liberty getting injured."

Issie frowned. "I think she can take care of herself."

Marcus shook his head. "The Valmont stables would freak out if they even knew Liberty was sharing her stall with another horse. They're very uptight about this mare. Mr Valmont doesn't even call her by her name – she's worth so much money that he refers to her as 'The Asset'."

"And they let you travel with her by yourself?"

"It was a last-minute thing. I was supposed to have Annie, my groom, with me to help out," Marcus said. "But Mr Valmont was short-staffed and kept her back at the stables. He's supposed to be hiring a new groom to meet up with me once I reach Kentucky. It's all right being on the road alone, though, I really don't mind."

"So you ride for this... Valmont Stables?" Issie asked.

"Uh-huh," Marcus said. "Valmont are a massive operation with lots of horses. I was considering moving back to England when my old riding instructor from boarding school phoned up and said she'd organised the ride on Liberty for me. That was six months ago and I've been working at the Valmont ranch in California ever since."

While Marcus slotted in the gate down the middle of the stall, Issie held on to Comet and Liberty. As soon as Marcus had locked the gate into place she let Comet loose in his stall, and then let Liberty go right next door.

Marcus looked at his watch. "Would you mind keeping an eye on her while she eats her feed? I better go back to my room and charge my mobile. I called Mr Valmont before to let him know where we are and the phone died. He likes to keep track of The Asset – he gets nervous if I don't call him while we're travelling."

"No problem," Issie said. "I've got to stay and make sure Comet settles in OK anyway."

"See you in the morning then?" Marcus said. "There's a diner just up the road. Maybe we can meet there for an early breakfast before we hit the road?"

"That sounds great," Issie said. "And thanks again for sharing Liberty's stall with me."

They watched as Comet craned his neck over the partition gate trying to get Liberty to notice him, but the mare steadfastly ignored his overtures and turned her rump on him so she was facing the corner of her stall.

"Give it up, Comet," Issie said as she turned out the light. "She's just not that into you."

Even with the curtains drawn shut in their room, Issie and Stella could still see the pink neon of the motel lights glowing softly outside in the forecourt. They had eaten pizza for dinner that evening with Avery.

"We've got a six a.m. start," Avery said as he scooped up the empty pizza boxes and headed for his room. "You girls should get some sleep."

As soon as the door was shut behind him Stella began

pressing the buttons on the TV remote, flicking through the endless channels. "Ohhh! There's a vampire versus werewolf movie marathon on channel forty-seven," she said. "Issie, we have to watch that!"

Issie knew they were supposed to get an early night, but if they were only going to be driving again tomorrow, surely it didn't matter how late they got to bed?

"All right," she agreed. "Turn it on then!"

"Wait!" Stella had an idea. "All those vampires will make us hungry – we need snacks!"

The vending machine in the motel forecourt was filled with strange sweets and chocolate that Issie and Stella had never heard of before. They pushed their coins into the slot and bought two Hersheys, a Butterfinger and a Peter Paul Almond Joy and took their chocolate haul back to their room.

"Imagine having to live on blood instead of chocolate," Stella said as she bit into the Almond Joy. "It must suck to be a vampire."

The movie marathon seemed like a good idea at the time, but the girls had underestimated just how tired they were. Stella was asleep within minutes, way before the first werewolf even appeared onscreen and Issie was left awake watching the TV.

The movie had just reached a particularly scary bit where the girl was all alone in the house and the werewolf was coming for her, when Issie heard the sound of an animal howling outside, somewhere in the darkness.

"Stella?" Issie hissed. "Did you hear that?"

Stella responded with a snore. Issie tried to pull herself together. She was imagining things. It was just one of the werewolves in the movie.

She'd almost convinced herself that this was true when she heard the noise again – definitely outside this time. It was a long, high-pitched howl, like a wild creature baying its heart out at the moon.

Probably a coyote, Issie thought. She recalled Avery saying that the hills around this region were full of them. As long as the coyote kept its distance and didn't bother the horses…

The coyote howled again and the motel lights outside flickered for a moment, and suddenly Issie had the strangest feeling. Something was out there – not far away in the hills, but right there – outside her room.

She could sense it somehow and it made the hairs stand up on the back of her neck.

Turning down the volume on the TV she got up out of her chair and padded silently towards the window. Issie held her breath as she slowly pulled back the curtain. The neon glow of the motel sign bathed the car park in pink light and at first Issie didn't see anything moving. She was about to let the curtain drop when she caught a glimpse of a shadowy shape heading towards her.

"Stella?" Issie hissed. "Stell? I think there's something out there!"

Issie looked back over her shoulder at her best friend who, despite everything, was still fast asleep. For a moment she considered waking her, but then she realised she would feel pretty stupid if it was just a stray dog outside.

Issie turned back to the window once more and immediately jumped back in fright. Right outside the room there were two coal-black eyes in a ghostly face, staring straight at her!

"Ohmygod!"

This was what happened when you watched silly movies! Issie had got herself totally freaked and had begun to imagine a werewolf lurking outside the window. What she hadn't been prepared for was a pony. But there he was, his snowy white coat taking on a pinkish glow from the neon light, making the sight of him strange and ghostly, but no less wonderful.

It was Mystic.

Chapter 4

Issie reached out and pressed her palm up against the glass.

"Hey, Mystic," she whispered to the dapple-grey pony. "It's good to see you."

Even as she said the words, though, Issie knew that Mystic's appearance in the middle of the night wasn't a good thing. The grey gelding only ever came when there was trouble. He'd come to warn her that something was very, very wrong.

Her thoughts focused immediately on Comet. Was the skewbald in danger? That coyote she'd heard howling could be closer than she thought. Would a coyote be bold enough to attack a horse?

Issie made a quick grab for her coat and headed out the door. She'd left Comet and Liberty with their feeds just a couple of hours ago. They'd both been fine when she'd said goodnight. She only hoped that they were still OK now.

Mystic was waiting for her right outside the door of her motel room. Her heart was racing as she reached his side. He nickered softly to her as she stretched out a hand to stroke his velvet-soft muzzle. "Hey, boy," she whispered to her pony, "it's been a long time." She put her arms round his neck, and pressed her face into the coarse, ropey strands of his long, silver-grey mane, hugging him tight. Mystic let out a tense whinny. He shook his head, freeing himself from her embrace. He flicked his head in agitation. They needed to go!

Suddenly the grey pony turned on his hocks and set off at a swift trot, heading across the motel forecourt, turning the corner round the end of the shell-pink motel buildings and veering round the back to the stables.

Issie sprinted after him, running as hard as she could, but the pony was too fast for her to keep up. By the time she rounded the corner into the courtyard behind the motel buildings, Mystic was already heading for the far end of the covered yards.

Plunged into the darkness of the yards, Issie suddenly found herself struggling to see anything at all. The lights had switched off automatically at 10 p.m. and the whole of the enclosure was in blackout.

"Mystic!" Issie hissed. "Where are you?"

As her eyes adjusted she could make out the silhouettes of horses in their stalls, moving about restlessly. Comet and Liberty's stall was at the very end of the yards and she headed there now, groping her way along the railings and trying to recall where the light switch had been. Then, in the blackness she thought she caught a glimpse of Mystic. He was pacing up and down beside Comet's stall and the skewbald was rearing and snorting, working himself up into a complete state, trying to get free. The rails were too tall for him to jump so he was skidding to a halt each time he reached the barrier, slamming against the wooden bars with his powerful chest, trying to force his way to freedom.

"Hey, hey! It's OK, Comet, I'm—" Issie was hurrying towards the skewbald when a dark figure suddenly rose up right in front of her. There was a man in the stalls!

Issie let out a shriek as the man clambered through the rails and barged into her, knocking her roughly to the ground.

Taken by surprise, she fell backwards. She threw out her hands to break her fall, but as she came down, her head struck hard against one of the wooden rails of the stall behind her. Her body slumped to the ground and everything went black.

Issie had no idea how long she was knocked out. All she knew was that when she woke up she was lying on the ground, with a massive throbbing pain in the back of her head and there was the dark shadow of a man standing over her. She tried to struggle to her feet and that was when she felt the bite of sharp metal against her chest. "Don't move!" she heard a voice say. There was a blinding glare as the stable lights flicked on and then she saw the face of Marcus Pearce staring down at her. He was shaking and wide-eyed as he stood with a pitchfork in his hands – the sharp prongs pressed against Issie's T-shirt, aiming directly at her heart.

"Marcus!" Issie couldn't believe it. "What are you doing?"

Marcus seemed just as shocked as Issie. He immediately dropped the pitchfork and extended a hand to help her back up again to her feet.

"I'm so sorry," Marcus said. "I didn't realise it was you. I heard noises and came out to check on the horses and thought I saw someone by the stalls. I grabbed that pitchfork to defend myself."

"There was somebody out here," Issie said as she dusted herself off. "A man was in with the horses. He knocked me over." She frowned at Marcus. "You didn't see him?"

Marcus shook his head. "You were the only one here when I arrived. Did you get a good look at him?"

"Not really," Issie admitted. "It was way too dark to make out his face."

"Are you OK?" Marcus asked. "You're not hurt?"

"I think I must have been knocked out for a minute," Issie said, "but I'm OK now, just a sore head."

"Are you sure you're all right?" Marcus asked.

"I'm fine," Issie insisted. "We'd better check the horses."

Comet and Liberty were still inside their stalls. Both

of them had clearly been terrified by the midnight intruder and they paced anxiously back and forth, refusing to calm down.

Issie stood on the other side of the railings and watched as Comet trembled and twitched, his head held high and the whites of his eyes showing, his nostrils flared wide. She felt exactly the same as her pony. Her heart refused to stop racing.

She calmed herself, taking some deep breaths, and it was only when she felt her pulse slowing at last that she knew she was ready to deal with the stressed-out Comet. She unbolted the gate and entered the stall, making her way slowly towards the skewbald. Comet was still freaked, but he was listening to her as she spoke to him, her voice a soft, lilting sing-song as she stepped closer to reassure him that it was all going to be OK, that he was safe, she was there with him. The skewbald let her get a hand on his halter and she clasped on the lead rope, leading him to the rail and tying him up so that she could run her hands down his legs, feeling for the heat or bump that would indicate an injury. She worked her way all over his body until she was satisfied that there was nothing wrong. Marcus, meanwhile, was in the stall beside her with Liberty, examining the mare.

"Comet's fine," she said to Marcus. "There's not a mark on him."

"Liberty looks OK too," Marcus confirmed. "But she's pretty shaken up."

He cast a worried gaze around the yard. "You know, I never thought about it before, but you could walk straight in here and steal a horse. The security at this place leaves a lot to be desired."

He looked at Issie. "What were you doing out here by yourself in the first place?"

"I heard noises too," Issie said. "I thought maybe it was coyotes." She didn't mention Mystic. She had figured out long ago that the pony was meant to be her secret, and by now the grey gelding was nowhere to be seen.

Marcus looked around the yard. Then he sat himself down on the hay bales in the corner next to Liberty's stall, took off his jacket and rolled it into a ball to make a pillow before he lay down.

"What are you doing?"

"I'm getting settled in for the night," Marcus said.

"There's always a chance that he'll come back, and I'm not leaving Liberty on her own. If anything happened to her then Mr Valmont would make sure I never worked at his stables again."

Marcus got himself comfy on the hay bale, tucking up his knees so his feet didn't dangle off the end. "You go inside," he told Issie. "Get some sleep. I'll keep an eye on them."

"Marcus, you can't stay out here by yourself…" Issie tried to change his mind.

"I'll be all right," Marcus said.

"But it's freezing!" Issie said.

"I'll be fine. Goodnight, Issie," Marcus replied firmly.

Issie went back to her room in a huff. If Marcus thought he was going to be a hero while she went back to her room and tucked herself into bed he had another think coming! She grabbed the blankets off her bed, and a pillow, plus two of the leftover chocolate bars from the vending machine, and went back outside.

"Who's there?" she heard Marcus call out as she walked back across the yards.

"It's me." Issie threw him one of the blankets along with a chocolate bar and then flopped down on a second hay bale alongside him. "You must be crazy if you think I'm leaving you here all alone. What if he comes back?"

Marcus picked up the chocolate bar. "I'll take the provisions, but I don't need the backup."

"You can't stop me sleeping out here," Issie said, plumping her pillow on top of the hay bale. "It's a free country."

Marcus was exasperated. "Are you always going to argue with everything I say?"

Issie chewed her chocolate bar thoughtfully. "Maybe."

Marcus laughed. "I think you just agreed with me. But I'm not sure."

"Goodnight, Marcus," Issie said, snuggling down under her blanket.

"Goodnight, Issie."

In the stall beside them Comet nickered softly, adding his own 'goodnight'. The skewbald craned his head over the rail and Issie felt his warm, horsey breath tickling her toes, which were sticking out from beneath the blanket.

"Comet! Quit it!"

The skewbald went back to nibbling at his hay net and Issie lay back and listened to the gentle sound of her pony's snorts as he chewed his hay, and before she knew it, she was fast asleep.

Aside from giving her the worst case of bed-hair that she'd ever had, Issie's hay bale proved to be a surprisingly good mattress. She woke up at dawn as the light came pouring into the yard. Marcus must have already gone back to his room. Issie checked Comet's hay net and water and then headed back to her room where Stella was waiting for her.

"You stayed out all night with Marcus Pearce?" Stella was stunned when Issie told her where she'd been.

"You make it sound like a date!" Issie said. "We both slept out in the stables to keep an eye on the horses because of the intruder."

"Issie!" Stella was horrified. "There's a stalker on the loose and you go off and hang out with Marcus, leaving me alone back here! Did you even think about me at all?"

Issie shook her head in disbelief. "Stella, I think you were safe. I'm pretty sure it was the horses that they were after."

"Well, you should have woken me," Stella sniffed. "You know I hate to miss out on stuff." She grabbed her coat. "Come on, we're meeting Tom at the diner for breakfast."

Avery and Marcus were occupying a booth together at the diner when the girls arrived. Marcus had already filled him in on the night's dramatic events.

"This can't have been a random attempt," Avery said. "The fact that they went straight for Comet and Liberty's stall makes me think that whoever this was, they knew our horses and they were targeting them."

Marcus shook his head. "No offence, Tom, I'm sure Comet is a terrific pony, but I don't think the horse thief was after him. The chances are far more likely that they were after Liberty. She's worth a lot of money."

Issie couldn't help feeling a little insulted by Marcus's comment. "Comet is worth a lot too," she told him. "I got offered twenty-five thousand dollars for him by Ginty McLintoch, and that was years ago. He must be worth at least five times that by now."

Marcus nodded politely and took a bite of his bagel. "Well I guess it depends on what you mean by a lot of money."

"Well what do *you* mean?" Issie asked him.

Marcus swallowed his bite and then said, "Mr Valmont has Liberty insured for three million dollars."

The whole table fell silent.

"Ohmygod!" Stella nearly choked on her toast. "If Liberty is worth that much then she should have been sleeping in the motel room and you should have been in the stables in the first place!"

"I know!" Marcus said. "That's why I said Mr Valmont would go berserk if anything happened to her."

Marcus raised his hand to wave to the waitress, who brought over a refill of coffee and his bill.

"I'm sorry," Marcus said, downing his coffee hastily and standing up. "I should get going. I'm supposed to make it to Little Rock by sunset. I'd better load Liberty up and head off."

He shook hands with Tom and then smiled at Issie. "I'll see you and Comet in Kentucky, OK?"

"Take care," Issie said, smiling back.

Stella's eyes flitted suspiciously as she noticed Issie watching Marcus leave the diner.

"Are you sure nothing romantic went on between you two?" she asked.

"Nothing happened, Stella," Issie groaned.

"Oh yeah?" Stella narrowed her gaze. "Then why do you have bits of hay bale stuck in your hair?"

"Duh, because I slept on a hay bale?" Issie rolled her eyes. "Honestly, Stella. There's nothing going on between me and Marcus Pearce."

Even as she said the words out loud, though, Issie knew that they weren't true. There was *something* between her and Marcus. From the moment they had met he had infuriated her!

"Marcus Pearce is the last boy on earth that I would ever get involved with," Issie said emphatically.

Years later, Stella would remind Issie of exactly what she'd said in the diner. But right now that future was still to come, and Issie had no idea how important Marcus Pearce would be, or that his horse would change her life forever.

Chapter 5

They spent two more days on the road, staying in horse motels. On Friday they spent the night in Arkansas where the motel had a round pen and a cattle yard, so Comet had a chance to stretch his legs. By Saturday they had reached Nashville, Tennessee, the country music capital of the United States. The motel here had theme rooms, each one dedicated to a different music icon. Avery had the Elvis room, while Issie and Stella had the Miley Cyrus room, which was decorated in various shades of bright pink with giant photographs of the singer all over the walls.

After the intruder at Rio Rancho, Issie was nervous about leaving Comet in the yards alone at night, but she figured that if there was any danger Mystic would alert her. As it turned out, both nights were uneventful and Issie slept undisturbed. Perhaps Marcus had been right when he said that the man in the stables that night had been after Liberty.

After three days of towing their dilapidated old horse float down the highways, and living off the fast food from the roadside diners, they were nearly at their destination.

"We'll be in Lexington by lunchtime," Avery announced as they drove down the main highway, past a sign that said *You're now leaving Nashville* in spangly gold writing beneath a giant cut-out shape of a silver guitar. "The Kentucky border is only a few hours away."

"If Nashville is famous for country music," Stella asked, "then what's Kentucky famous for?"

"Racehorses," Avery said. "There are over five hundred horse farms in the Lexington district alone."

It was just before midday when Avery took the highway exit to Route 64 and they began to head into bluegrass country. Issie looked out the windows at the sprawling miles of white post-and-rail surrounding green pastureland. It was April and the dogwood trees were in bloom. In the fields the mares grazed with their young foals at foot. Most of the colts and fillies were still only a few months old and too young to be separated from their mums.

"It's so beautiful around here," Issie said, staring out the window as they passed yet another racehorse farm, an elegant white Southern mansion surrounded by red barns. "It's like horse heaven."

This was heartland horse country, home to some of the wealthiest Thoroughbred stud farms in the world and the Kentucky Horsepark was right in the middle of it. At first you couldn't tell the horsepark apart from the rest of the surrounding farms. It was fenced exactly the same as the other properties, with endless miles of white post-and-rail. The difference was the horses. Kentucky Horsepark had some Thoroughbreds grazing in their fields, but they shared the pastures with exotic breeds from all around the globe.

"Ohmygod!" Stella wound down the window of the Jeep to get a better look at the horses. "Look! Aren't they cute!"

A herd of multicoloured miniature ponies in every colour from piebald to palomino had their heads down in the long grass right beside the road. Their diminutive size made them look comical alongside the massive Percheron draught horse grazing nearby, towering above them like a gentle giant. In the field alongside the Percheron a jet-black horse with feathered legs and a flowing curly mane raised his head to watch the horse float drive by. "That is the most beautiful Friesian I have ever seen!" Stella said.

"They have over forty rare breeds at the Kentucky Horsepark," Avery explained as they passed another field with spotted appaloosas and golden palomino Quarter Horses grazing without any rugs, their coats shining in the Kentucky sunshine.

They didn't take the main entrance to the park. Instead, Avery turned down a side road signposted as Nina Bonnie Boulevard. They drove on until they reached another gateway where a tall stand of clipped conifers marked the entrance and the sign at the gate read: *Access For Competitors Only*.

Halfway down the avenue there was a security gate with a guard posted beside it. Avery took off the lanyard that he was wearing round his neck and showed it to the guard, who examined it and gave them directions before letting them through.

"He says that the stables are just up ahead to the right," Avery said. "Comet's stall is in Block C."

"This place is totally massive!" Stella leant out the window to stare at the rows of loose boxes.

"The park has stabling for three hundred horses," Avery explained. "Horses must remain on site the whole time while the competition is underway."

He pulled the float up in a parking bay beside the stable block with the giant letter 'C' painted on the front wall.

"This will be Comet's home for the next week. We're going to be staying nearby in the competition village. I've booked us two cabins."

Avery pointed in the direction of the village, but Issie was looking out towards the green fields – she'd just caught her first glimpse of the cross-country course that she would be riding in four days' time.

She could make out a couple of the jumps. There was a vast trakehner and one of the water complexes. Even from this distance she could see that the fences were far bigger than anything she'd ever ridden before.

"When will we get the chance to walk the course?" she asked Avery, feeling the butterflies suddenly taking up residence in her tummy.

"On Wednesday," Avery said. "The course is out of bounds until then. After that you can walk it on foot as many times as you like, but horses aren't allowed near the course until they compete. You can ride in any of the indoor schooling arenas that are marked with an X," Avery said, passing her a fold-out map. "The big building is the dressage complex – that's where you'll be competing on Friday in your test. And those are the showjumping arenas where you'll be riding the final phase on the Sunday."

"Wow," Stella said, pointing to a flashy silver horse truck, "check that out!"

The truck was enormous – big enough to take at least six horses, and totally sleek and glamorous. Issie suddenly felt awfully self-conscious parked next to it with their rust-bucket horse float. Their arrival was certainly drawing a few strange sideways glances from the grooms in the stable yard. She watched as one groom walked past with a glossy chestnut gelding dressed in smart white bandages with a perfectly pulled mane and she thought about Comet, her loveable but scruffy 14.2 skewbald that she had brought to compete on. Was she kidding herself? Maybe this competition really was out of her league.

Issie's feelings of being out of place weren't helped when a brunette in khaki chinos emerged from the office at the end of the stable block and walked briskly over towards them as they were preparing to unload Comet.

"I'm sorry," the woman said, shaking her head, "but you can't park your horse float here. This area is for eventing competitors only."

Avery held up his lanyard tag that he had shown to the guard at the gate. "We are competitors," he said. 'This is Isadora Brown. She's entered on her pony, Blackthorn Comet."

The woman was shocked. "I'm so sorry!" she said, looking deeply embarrassed as she stepped forward to shake Avery's hand. "I didn't realise. Welcome to Kentucky Horsepark. You must be Mr Avery. I'm Blaire Andrews, I'm the manager of these stables."

Blaire coughed, still looking rather embarrassed. "I'll wait while you unload Blackthorn Comet and then I can show you to your loose box and give you the tour of our facilities."

If Blaire Andrews had been shocked by the state of the horse float, the look on her face when she saw the pony inside it was priceless. You could see she was holding her tongue as she watched Issie backing the little skewbald out of the float.

Comet came high-stepping down the ramp, raised his head up and gave a look-at-me whinny, as if to say "I've arrived, everyone!"

"Well isn't he a friendly little guy! I can see he's quite a character!" Blaire said, trying to be positive, but clearly not entirely convinced that this pony was really Four-Star material. "I have Comet's stall ready and waiting if you want to bring him this way?"

Avery, Stella, Issie and Comet followed behind Blaire as she led them past the elegant rows of loose boxes.

"You've arrived just in time," Blaire told them as they walked. "The meet-and-greet is tonight."

"What's that?" Stella asked.

"It's a chance for the riders to get to know each other before the event begins," Blaire explained. "You'll find your tickets and all the details in the competitors' orientation kit I've prepared for you. The event is in the museum at six."

Comet's loose box was one of the last ones in the long row of almost thirty stalls in stable block C.

"It's got state-of-the-art technology," Blaire said,

swiping her passcard through an electronic monitor beside the door. "Riders, trainers and their teams are assigned their own passcards to ensure that horses are secure at all times."

She pointed out the features of the stall. "There are thermostats to keep the climate regular, surfaces are hypo-allergenic, including the straw bedding, and water troughs fill automatically."

As Blaire listed the features of his new stall, Comet was already snuffling about in the feed bin that was hanging on the wall in the hope that there might be some tidbits in there.

They left the skewbald in his stall while they continued the tour. Issie wanted to give her pony a hug goodbye, but with Blaire standing by watching her, she decided it would look unprofessional – Four-Star eventing riders didn't do that sort of thing, did they? And so she settled for a slappy pat on Comet's neck before leaving him in his new temporary home.

The stable blocks each had their own hose-down areas, tack rooms and electronic horse-walking machines. There was a horse swimming pool to the rear of the complex for all the horses to use, and a feed bin room where grains and chaff were kept and the special dietary needs for each horse were catalogued on wall charts for the grooms to follow.

After touring the stables, Blaire walked them through blocks, D, E, F, G and H until they had come out the other side of the stables and were in the riders' village.

"You've got cabins two-four-one and three-two-three." Blaire gave one cabin key to Avery and one to Issie and Stella.

The cabins were small, self-contained units with twin beds and a bathroom. Issie was dying to collapse on her bed as the dreaded jetlag had struck yet again, but she knew there wasn't time. They had to unpack their bags right away and get changed for the meet-and-greet.

It was nearly 6 p.m. when Avery came to meet them at their cabin and they walked together back through the stables, checking in on Comet, using their new passcards to visit his stall before continuing on towards the main buildings of the Horsepark.

There was a Stars and Stripes flag flying in front of the entrance to the museum and over the doorway a gold banner read: *Welcome Competitors to The Kentucky Four-Star Three-Day Event.*

In the foyer there was a table with name tags arranged on it for the guests. Not that most of the riders needed to wear them – Issie recognised their famous faces by sight. New Zealand riders Andrew Nicholson and Mark Todd were helping themselves to a tray of club sandwiches while British equestriennes Daisy Berkeley and Mary King stood nearby chatting.

"Ohmygod!" Stella suddenly took in a sharp gasp of breath and grabbed at Issie's arm as if she'd just seen Justin Bieber. "Is that Oliver Townend over there? He's so cool! And look, there's Pippa Funnell!"

Issie couldn't believe it. She had ridden against a few of these riders at Three-Star circuits in Europe, but she'd never seen so many equestrian super-celebrities together in one room before.

"Look!" Issie hissed in Stella's ear. "Over there! It's Paul Tapner!"

The dashing, dark-haired winner of the Badminton Horse Trials was chatting away to a fellow Australian, Clayton Fredericks and his wife, Lucinda.

There was a fourth rider standing with the Australians. He had his back to Issie and Stella and at first they couldn't see who he was, but a moment later he turned round and when he caught sight of the girls his smile lit up the room.

"Hey!" he said. "Fancy seeing you guys here!"

Stella's jaw dropped open. "Ohmygod!"

It was Shane Campbell, former captain of the Australian junior team and Stella's one-time boyfriend!

"What are you doing here?" Issie asked. "I never saw your name on the list for Kentucky!"

"Bruce McDonald's horse pulled a ligament so I replaced him on the Australian team," Shane said. "I'm going to be riding against you in the Four-Star! Cool, huh?"

"Totally!" Issie said. She was pleased to see Shane – but at the same time her competitive streak made her assess him as a real danger. Shane was a really good rider and he already had some experience riding Four-Star – he'd gone clear on the cross-country at Adelaide in Australia last November on his talented mare, Queen Latifah.

"I could use a groom if you're available, Stella?" Shane said, giving her a cheeky grin.

"Sorry," Stella smiled back, "I'm Team Issie."

"Maybe I can change your mind over dinner?" Shane

said, flirting shamelessly with her. "Maybe you and I could go get some food after the meet-and-greet is over?"

"I'd love to—" Stella began but Avery interrupted her.

"—but she can't." He finished Stella's sentence. "Stella has an early start tomorrow morning at six to get Comet ready for his first day of training. I'm sorry, Shane. I'm sure she'll have time to catch up with you after the competition is over, but the girls are on a nine p.m. curfew until then."

"You're kidding me!" Stella was wide-eyed.

"Do I look like I'm kidding?" Avery asked.

"So what happens if I'm not back to my room before nine?" Stella pouted. "Do I turn into a pumpkin?"

"No," Avery deadpanned, "you turn into an unemployed groom."

Stella looked furious, but Shane could see that they weren't going to talk Avery around. "It's OK," he said. "We can catch up tomorrow and have lunch maybe?"

"Sure," Stella said. She was trying to act cool, but her flushed cheeks and shining eyes showed just how thrilled she was to see Shane Campbell again. She'd never quite got over the boy she'd described as "the world's best kisser"!

"It's almost like a Havenfields reunion tonight," Shane continued, referring to the farm where they'd first met when Stella and Issie had travelled to Melbourne to compete in the Express Eventing Challenge. "There's you guys and me… and Tara."

"Tara?" Issie was shocked. "Tara Kelly is here?"

"Yeah," Shane nodded. "I saw her just a moment ago. Hey, there she is! Tara!"

He gave a wave across the room and a cool, elegant woman with walnut-brown hair, wearing cream jodhpurs and a white blouse, waved back and came over to join them.

"Issie, Stella and – oh my goodness, Tom Avery!" Tara smiled warmly as she embraced her old friend. "How good to see you in Lexington!"

"You too!" Issie grinned. "I didn't expect to see you here."

"Well, it's hardly that surprising, is it?" Tara said. "I do live here, after all."

Tara Kelly had once been a world-famous eventing rider, but by the time Issie met her she had given up competing in favour of teaching. Tara wasn't just a teacher, however, she was also the chief talent scout for the legendary Blainford "All-Stars" Academy – an elite equestrian boarding school in Lexington, Kentucky.

Tara had once offered Issie a place as a pupil at her school – and although Issie had turned it down, there was no bad blood between them. In fact, Issie was thrilled to run into Tara once more.

"So why are you at this meet-and-greet?" Avery asked. "Don't tell me you're thinking about coming out of retirement and riding in the Four-Star?"

Tara shook her head. "My riding days are well and truly behind me, Tom."

"Tara's already won Lexington three times!" Issie pointed out. "She needs to give the rest of us a chance!"

Tara smiled. "That's very kind of you, Issie, but I think I should warn you that I'm not leaving the field completely open. One of my former star pupils from Blainford is competing. I'm here as his trainer."

"And who is this former pupil?" Avery asked.

"Ah," Tara looked around the room. "Last time I saw him he was stuck talking to that awful blabbermouth Tiggy Brocklebent from *Horsing Around* magazine. I'll go and save him from her clutches and bring him over. I'll be back in a moment…"

Tara sashayed off through the crowd and a few seconds later she returned with her young protégé in tow.

"Now," Tara said brightly, "allow me to do the introductions…"

Issie shook her head. "Ummm, Tara, actually you don't need to introduce us."

Tara frowned. "What do you mean?"

The young rider standing next to Tara spoke up. "She means we've already met."

"You've met?"

"Uh-huh," the young man said with a grin.

Tara Kelly's young protégé was none other than Marcus Pearce.

Chapter 6

With the Four-Star event just a few days from getting underway, all the competitors had arrived. By 6 a.m. on Monday morning the stables were frantic with activity as the grooms began their daily routine: feeding and watering the horses, mucking out the stalls and preparing for the day ahead.

Issie and Stella were among those making an early start. They had no trouble getting out of bed after their super-early night – but Stella wasn't happy about turning down Shane's offer.

"Shane will go off me completely," she grumbled. "He's probably already met another rider who doesn't have a curfew – someone fabulous and gorgeous!"

"Shane isn't interested in anyone fabulous and gorgeous," Issie said. "He likes you."

"Thanks!" Stella said sarcastically.

"Oh, you know what I mean!" Issie said. She'd been dying to stay at the party too. Her conversation with Marcus and Tara had been all too brief – she would have loved to stay and hear more about life at Blainford Academy. Marcus had just left the school last year. He'd been Tara's star pupil, earning himself top honours in the eventing senior class.

"The Valmont stables are always waiting to snap up my best graduates," Tara said.

"I was lucky," Marcus said modestly.

"No, they were fortunate to get you," Tara insisted. "And I'll be telling Mr Valmont that in person when he arrives."

"He's coming here to watch you ride?" Issie asked.

Marcus groaned. "As if I needed more pressure!"

"The Valmont stables have great hopes for the mare that Marcus is riding," Tara said. "Liberty is a real athlete with magnificent bloodlines, superb breeding and schooling." She smiled at Issie. "Anyway, tell me about your mount for Lexington."

"I'm riding Comet," Issie said. "A fourteen-two hand high hill country pony from my Aunty Hester's farm in Gisborne."

Tara frowned. "No, seriously. What are you riding?"

Comet might not have sounded like much of a prospect to Tara. He lacked breeding and class, but he made up for it with strength of character and raw talent – or at least that was what Issie thought. Her only concern about Comet was the dressage phase. He'd never been the most enthusiastic dressage pony, often getting bored with trotting around in circles when he could be jumping. However, during the past year at Laurel Farm the skewbald had been given extensive dressage schooling by Francoise D'Arth. Francoise had ridden as one of the members of the famed *Cadre Noir de Saumur* riding school, and had also been the head dressage instructor at *El Caballo Danza Magnifico* Stables in Andalusia. For three long months Francoise despaired of ever making progress, and had pronounced that Comet was unteachable.

But then, one morning after a schooling session, she came into the kitchen at Laurel Farm smiling cheerfully. "We've made a breakthrough!" she told Issie. "All those months he acts like a buffoon and then today out of nowhere he does a perfect half-pass! It is like he read the entire dressage manual overnight. All of a sudden he seems to know the high-school moves – he is performing beautifully."

It wasn't just Francoise's schooling that gave Issie confidence in Comet. She knew the skewbald's nature. The little pony was fiercely competitive and a dreadful show-off. Issie just knew that the moment he found himself in front of the huge crowd of spectators in the main arena at Kentucky, Comet would raise his game. The pony loved performing for an audience and the bigger the crowd, the better he would be.

Issie had anticipated that Avery would want to work on their dressage test today and so she'd helped Stella to tack the pony up in his dressage saddle and bridle. But when Avery arrived at the stalls he had other plans.

"I don't think Comet is in the right headspace yet,"

Avery told Issie. "He's been cooped up during all the travelling we've been doing and he's tense and bored. He's likely to blow up in the arena and you'll end up in a fight with him."

Avery turned to Stella. "Take off the dressage saddle and tack him up in the cross-country saddle instead. Issie – can you go and put your back protector on? I've booked the racetrack for the next hour."

"The racetrack?" Issie was confused. "Tom, Comet is not a racehorse!"

"No," Avery agreed, "but he needs a good gallop. The cross-country course is off limits so the racetrack was the next best option."

Avery legged Issie up on to Comet's back and walked alongside her, leading the way through the stables to the northern fields where the training track was located. It was a broad strip of soft loamy soil, bordered on either side by white rails, just like a professional galloping track.

"So you want us to gallop?" Issie asked as Comet

began to grab at the bit and sidestep like a crab in his eagerness to get moving.

"Not straight away," Avery warned her. "He needs to get loosened up first, so give him a couple of circuits at the trot to get his muscles warm, then you can give him a good gallop to clear his wind."

Issie set off round the track at a brisk trot, posting up and down in the saddle. Comet was a bit spooky at first, eyeing up a rubbish bin and skipping sideways as they rode past, as if the bin were going to come alive and eat him. But by the time they had completed a circuit the skewbald was in a totally upbeat mood and trotting rhythmically, the soft thud of his hooves on the sandy loam setting a steady beat.

"OK, take him up into a gallop now," Avery instructed.

It was Issie's first time back in the saddle on Comet since they'd left England, and she worried that the week of travelling might have knocked the skewbald's fitness levels. Back at Laurel Farm she had spent the past few months working hard to get Comet fit enough to make it round the gruelling six-kilometre cross-country course in Kentucky. She'd given the pony regular interval training, trotting and cantering him through the forests that surrounded the farm, vital fitness work to prepare him for the cross-country. It was especially important for Comet since the 14.2 hand pony would have his work cut out for him rivalling the pace and endurance of the other horses who were full-sized hacks.

Had Issie done enough to keep him in top condition or had the past week in transit taken too much of a toll on the skewbald? As she eased him into a gallop and popped up into two-point position, balancing on her knees over the withers, she felt the pony beneath her answer the question almost immediately as he powered around the track, his strides eating up the ground.

The wind stung her face, and Issie's eyes began to stream tears as she came around to finish her first lap at a gallop. A full circuit of the racetrack was over a kilometre, enough to tire a racehorse, but Comet came past the post without breaking a sweat. Issie sat up a little in the saddle to slow him, but Comet didn't want to stop now. He continued to pull on the reins, demanding to be let loose so that he could go faster. Watching from the sidelines Avery waved Issie on to go around again. She gave him a nod then leant down low over Comet's neck and urged the skewbald on.

She was balanced up above the withers, rocking in perfect rhythm with the pony beneath her as they completed the second circuit. Avery waved them on again, and Issie actually clucked the pony and put her legs on to ask for even more speed. Comet responded without hesitation, and the thunder of his hooves on the track became faster and louder, pounding like the blood in Issie's veins as they stretched out in full gallop. They had ridden three kilometres when they passed the marker once more and this time Avery signalled with his hands to slow down. Issie sat back in the saddle and strengthened her grip on the reins. The pony was snorting and trembling from the thrill of the run and at first she had trouble convincing him, but she spoke softly to Comet and eventually the skewbald trotted, before taking a final lap at a walk to cool down. By the time they came back to join Avery Comet was swinging along with his ears pricked forward and looked keen to do it all over again.

Avery looked pleased. "He's fitter than he's ever been."

Issie dismounted and ran up her stirrups. "He felt great out there. You were right Tom, he just needed to blow the cobwebs out. He's ready for this – I can feel it."

Comet was much more settled by the next morning and when Avery arrived at the stables he instructed Stella to tack the skewbald up in his dressage gear ready for a solid schooling session.

Issie mounted up and Avery walked alongside her as they headed out to the arena, outlining his plan for the final three days of training before the competition began.

"We'll do some schooling today, but let's not run through the actual dressage test. Comet is smart and we don't want him to learn the sequences off by heart, or he'll anticipate your next movement and may change paces too soon. I've booked the showjumping arena tomorrow for three p.m., and we'll pop him over a course with a lot of twists and turns just to get you both in the groove again. Then on Thursday he can have a light schooling session after he's passed the trot-up…"

Avery's sentence trailed off as he looked over towards the dressage arenas and saw Tara Kelly and Marcus with Liberty saddled up and ready. Standing beside them was a distinguished-looking middle-aged man in a pinstripe suit.

"Looks like Liberty's owner has arrived," Avery said.

Mr Valmont was not alone. Two men, both dressed in suits and wraparound sunglasses, stood back and waited behind him while he talked with Tara and Marcus.

As Issie and Avery walked past with Comet, Tara called them over and did the introductions. "Tom Avery and Isadora Brown – this is Mr Valmont."

"Call me Tyrel," Valmont said as he shook hands with Avery.

Issie noticed that the hand extended to Avery was perfectly manicured and a diamond-studded watch hung round its wrist. Everything about Tyrel Valmont oozed wealth and success, from his sleek silver-grey hair, to his sparkling white teeth and tanned skin.

He exposed those perfect teeth now as he smiled at Issie. "I think I owe you a debt of thanks, young lady. Marcus was just telling me that you had a hand in keeping my mare out of trouble in Rio Rancho."

"I'm just glad that she's safe," Issie said.

"So am I," Valmont said. He looked at Liberty. "This mare is a key asset in my stables and I wouldn't want anything else to go wrong." Valmont looked sternly at Marcus. "There's no reason why we shouldn't be taking home the Four-Star trophy on Sunday, is there, Marcus? I expect you to go double-clear on The Asset in the cross-country and the showjumping, otherwise it might be time for you to start looking for a new stable to work for."

"Uhhh, no, sir. I mean, yes, sir," Marcus said nervously.

A mobile phone rang and one of Valmont's men answered it and then came over and whispered something to his boss.

"It appears I am required in a meeting," Mr Valmont said.

"Don't you have time to stay and watch Marcus ride Liberty?" Tara asked.

Valmont looked at his watch. "OK," he said. "But make it quick!"

When they reached the dressage arena Marcus began to warm up the mare, but Valmont shook his head. "I'm not paying you to trot her in circles, son," he said. "Let's see some one-time canter changes now, please!"

"But the mare hasn't been warmed up yet," Tara objected.

"I appreciate your interest in my horses, trainer," Valmont said coolly, "but it would pay for you to remember that I'm the one in charge here."

Tara fell into stunned silence and Valmont turned his attention back to Marcus. "That's a three-million-dollar mare you're riding," he shouted out to him, "and you're treating her like a cart horse. Get her going!"

Issie was shocked by Valmont's rudeness. She saw a look of annoyance cross Marcus's face, but he didn't argue. He did exactly what Mr Valmont demanded, urging Liberty on into a fabulous collected canter straight down the long side of the arena, before turning the mare down the diagonal to do a series of flying changes through the centre of the arena. Issie could tell that Marcus was feeling a bit flustered and the changes were a bit ragged. Liberty wasn't quite ready and her muscles and her mind hadn't been warmed up properly. Horses were just like any other athletes – they needed to limber up and prepare for difficult tricks, like endless flying changes. All the same, it was an amazing effort and Issie was blown away as she watched Liberty perform. The mare was so beautiful and Marcus had clearly worked long and hard to develop a solid partnership with her. She wasn't an easy horse to ride, that was obvious, but when he got her going properly she looked stunning.

Valmont, however, was less impressed. "If I was scoring you on that I'd give you a six," he told Marcus flatly as he brought the mare to a halt. "I expect every performance to be a nine or a ten with a horse like Liberty. Sharpen up your act!"

This time Issie really thought that Marcus was going to say something back to his boss, but he was saved by a mobile phone ringing as one of Valmont's men took another call and then interrupted them again. "I'm sorry, Mr Valmont," he said. "That was your next meeting. They say they can't wait any longer."

"Right," Mr Valmont said. He shook hands briskly with Tara. "You've got lots to work on, haven't you?" he told her. "I'll be back on Friday to watch the dressage and we'll talk then."

And with that, Valmont strode off across the arena heading for the gates with his men following dutifully behind him.

"Right!" Tara said briskly to Marcus after Valmont had departed. "Shall we get to work on those one-time changes?"

Marcus shook his head. "I think Liberty and I have both had enough for today," he said darkly. And before Tara could argue with him, he'd vaulted down off Liberty and was leading the mare back towards the stables.

For the rest of the morning Issie practised her dressage workout on Comet, also focusing hard on canter one-time changes and pirouettes, and by the end of the session both she and Comet were dripping with sweat and exhausted. Issie had handed the reins over to Stella to take Comet to the hose-down bay and she was walking back towards the rider's village when she saw Marcus. He was heading towards Liberty's stall and Issie could see instantly by the expression on his face that he still had a thundercloud hanging over his head after that morning's episode with Valmont.

"Hey!" Issie called out and ran to catch him up.

Marcus gave her a half-hearted smile. "Hi, Issie."

Issie smiled back. "I just wanted to say that I thought it was pretty harsh, you know, the way Valmont treated you."

"Yeah, he's not exactly the kind of guy who cheers you up when he visits," Marcus said. They had been walking through the stable block as they were talking and had reached Liberty's stall. Marcus pulled his passcard out of his pocket to access the mare's loose box and Issie noticed that he had a different-coloured card to hers. Her card was blue, coded to match the colour of the 'C' stable block whereas Marcus had a green card to match stable block 'D'.

"I don't think I could work for a man like Valmont," Issie said.

"Yeah, he's a total jerk," Marcus agreed. "I can't tell you how many times I've had the conversation in my mind where I shout back and tell him that I quit." He sighed. "But he's the boss. And he has some amazing horses. It's a huge opportunity to ride for Valmont Stables."

"Is he always like that?" Issie asked.

"It's got worse lately," Marcus admitted. "He's under a lot of stress and I guess he's been through a lot lately. Especially the whole tragedy with Valmont Promise."

Issie didn't know what he was talking about.

"You never heard about it?" Marcus said. "It was in all the newspapers last year."

Issie shook her head. "Who is Valmont Promise?"

"Promise was Valmont's superstar," Marcus explained. "He was the best horse in his stables. One of those special horses, you know? All the grooms and the riders loved him. He had an amazing temperament and he was so beautiful – a Thoroughbred, but really solidly built – almost seventeen hands. He was the dream eventer – so talented…" Marcus trailed off. "Anyway, Promise was competing at his first big three-day event in California. He was halfway round the cross-country when he fell…".

"He hit a jump?" Issie asked.

Marcus shook his head. "No, it was so weird, he wasn't anywhere near a jump. He was in the final stretch on the way home, and one minute he was galloping, totally fine, and the next he'd just collapsed on the track. The vet arrived a few moments later and said he must have had a massive heart attack."

"So was he OK? Did he finish the competition?" Issie asked.

"No, Issie, you don't understand. By the time the vet had reached him, there was nothing he could do," Marcus said. "Valmont Promise was dead."

Chapter 7

The sudden death of Valmont Promise haunted Issie. She kept thinking about how awful it must have been for Promise's poor rider to feel his horse suddenly collapse beneath him. To start out on the cross-country course so full of hope and excitement only to have it end in tragedy.

Promise's death was not the first time that a horse had died on a cross-country course. Eventing was a deadly sport, and Issie was reminded all too clearly of just how real the risks were on Wednesday morning as she stood with Tom at the start line of the cross-country course and prepared to walk it for the first time.

When you watch a three-day event on the television the fences look big. But when you are actually walking the course they aren't big – they're humungous. The first three fences weren't too bad, but when Issie faced up to the fourth fence, a set of rails placed diagonally over a ditch known as 'the Bridge', she felt her mouth go dry in horror. If she stood at the point where the horses would be taking off then she couldn't even see over the bridge to the other side. The jump was taller than her! And it wasn't just the height of the fence that was terrifying, it was the spread as well. At the point where the horses would take off, the bridge was over two metres wide. But it wasn't even the widest fence on the course. The biggest spread came towards the end of the course at fence 24, the Gamekeeper's Brush. The brush had a ditch in front of it that the horses needed to clear, which made the total spread of the jump a massive 2.7 metres wide!

"It's what they call a 'rider frightener'," Avery pointed out to her. "Comet will clear that ditch easily – he won't even notice that it's there as long as *you* look up and focus on the brush ahead; that's the key. If you look down, then you'll go down."

They had taken nearly two hours to reach fence 24. Avery liked to walk a course slowly the first time so that he could examine everything in detail, pacing out the number of strides between the elements and checking the terrain for any hidden problems that might arise.

Issie, meanwhile, had been just as busy checking out the other competitors. Since the course had only just been opened that morning it was swarming with riders. Issie watched as the famed Austrian eventer Gerhardt Muller and his trainer strolled from fence to fence, chatting gaily as they walked. Gerhardt was so lanky and tall he could virtually throw his legs over the fences himself. He seemed self-assured as he eyed up the stride into the Gamekeeper's Brush and stepped out his line. Issie, on the other hand, couldn't even think about the striding – all she could think about was the size of that enormous ditch! It was big and deep enough to bury her and Comet if they mis-stepped and plunged into it.

Not that the Gamekeeper's Brush was Issie's only concern. She was also worried about the two water jumps. The first one, the Duck Marsh, had a giant wooden carved duck sitting in the middle of the water jump – the horses literally had to leap over the duck's back.

"You'll have to ride precisely at the duck," Avery agreed. "It's a narrow fence, but Comet is fine with narrow fences."

"He's never jumped a duck before!" Issie pointed out.

Avery shook his head. "He's a horse, Issie. As far as he's concerned, that jump is just another obstacle to be cleared. Comet doesn't know that he's jumping over a duck."

The giant duck wasn't the only strange animal on the course. Fences 17 and 18 had wooden carvings in the shape of gigantic squirrels sitting upright on their hindquarters with their brushy tails extending out behind them to act as hedges.

"Remember to aim for the dead centre of the squirrel tail," Avery told her.

"Now there's a sentence I never thought I'd hear," Issie said, managing a feeble, nervous grin.

Many of the fences on the course had alternative routes for the riders to take. These alternatives were always longer and chewed up valuable seconds on the clock, which could lead to time faults, but they were also easier and safer options so the horses were more likely to go clear if they took the easy path. Many of the more experienced riders were choosing the longer, safer options – especially at tricky fences like the first squirrel jump, where riders were allowed to veer left and take another small fence that would set them up with a better line to the second squirrel.

Avery, however, dismissed the notion of the longer routes, saying that it would add too much time.

"You go straight through," he told Issie. "Comet is a clever and honest jumper – he can handle the tough options, but he's also much smaller than the other horses so you're going to be cutting it fine when it comes to time. You cannot afford to waste a single second. You must stick to the short route between every jump, no matter what."

It took them three hours to walk the course. It was funny, Issie thought, that what had taken her and Avery so long would be over in a matter of minutes on the big day. The optimum time for riding the cross-country was set at sixteen minutes and ten seconds – and any riders who exceeded this would get time penalties added on to their scores.

By the time they reached the final fence, the Bourbon Barrels, they had been caught up by several other riders, including Tara Kelly and Marcus.

"What did you think of it?" Marcus asked Issie as they walked back together to the stables.

"It was bigger than I expected it to be," Issie admitted, hoping that her voice wouldn't betray her nervousness. She was having a flashback to the ditch in front of the Gamekeeper's Brush. If it was intended as a rider frightener then the course designer had done his job nicely – she was terrified by it!

"The water jumps are going to cause a few crashes, I think," Marcus said. "I'm worried about the Normandy Bank towards the end. Liberty is a big striding mare and the distance between the fences is quite tight."

"Not for Comet's little legs, it isn't," Issie laughed.

"I'm going to walk it again tomorrow morning straight after breakfast before the trotting-up," Marcus said. "You want to come with me?"

"Sounds great," Issie agreed. "Meet you then."

Issie wanted to walk the course at least three times before the cross-country took place on Saturday. She could walk it on Thursday morning with Marcus and then one final time on the Friday afternoon with Avery once she'd done her dressage test. The rules of the three-day event allowed riders to walk the course as many times as they liked and some of them would walk it as many as four or five times. The horses, on the other hand, were not permitted to see the jumps until they were on the course competing, so they would be looking at the fences in front of them with totally fresh eyes. Of course, there was nothing in the rules to stop Issie telling Comet all about the course.

"The jumps are very big, Comet," Issie told the little skewbald when she arrived back at the stables, "but then we knew they were going to be, didn't we?"

Comet nickered back in agreement. Issie grabbed a body brush out of his grooming kit and began to brush the skewbald's patchy chestnut and white face.

"There's a really big spread at jump twenty-four, the Gamekeeper's Brush," she whispered to the pony. "I'm a bit freaked out by it, but I…"

"Hey! What are you doing?"

It was Stella and she looked cross.

"If you keep brushing and feeding Comet then Avery will notice I have nothing to do and send me home," Stella said, taking the body brush out of Issie's hand and shaking her head. "Being the groom is my job, Issie – you've got enough to do."

Issie knew this was true. Looking after Comet was officially Stella's role. But Issie had never really got used to the idea of having a groom.

"I feel like a spoilt princess," Issie complained.

"There's nothing stuck-up about having a groom," Stella pointed out. "It's just professional, that's all. The whole point of having me to do this stuff is to free you up so that you can focus on competing. You've got enough on your plate."

She looked at her watch. "Like, aren't you due at the rider briefing in five minutes?"

Avery was looking decidedly twitchy when Issie rushed into the media room.

Where have you been? her trainer mouthed at her as she pushed her way through the crowds to take a seat beside him. Issie plonked herself down just as Blaire Andrews stepped up to the lectern at the front of the room and tapped on the microphone to check it was on.

"Good afternoon, everyone," she smiled. "Thank you so much for coming today. With just one more day before the Kentucky Four-Star gets underway this final briefing session is intended to cover all the key issues and any last-minute concerns that riders might have.

We'd also like to use this opportunity for all of you to meet the press…"

"Yoo hoo!" Issie looked up to the left of the room where a plump blonde woman dressed in Donegal tweed was frantically waving. The blonde woman pushed past a couple of other riders at the back and crammed herself into the spare seat on the other side of Issie.

"We haven't met before," the woman whispered hoarsely, trying to keep her voice down as Blaire Andrews explained the rules regarding the trotting-up. "I'm Tiggy Brocklebent, senior writer at *Horsing Around* magazine." She extended a chubby hand for Issie to shake. "I'd love to do an interview with you, for my magazine."

"Ummmm, yeah, sure…" Issie frowned. She had just missed what Blaire had said. It was something about being disqualified at the trotting-up if you didn't have the right number on your horse.

"You're the youngest rider *ever* to compete at Lexington, did you realise that?" Tiggy continued in her throaty whisper. "When I saw your name on the list of riders I said to my editor – now there's our story! And you're riding a fourteen-two pony? Unbelievable stuff, I'd—"

"Ummm, Tiggy?" Issie whispered back. "Can we talk after the rider briefing? I really need to hear this."

"Absolutely!" Tiggy said, "I was just saying earlier to Caroline Powell... do you know Caroline? You must know her! You're both from New Zealand. She lives in the UK too – just like you do. Such a lovely woman! It was such a thrill when she won the Burghley Horse Trials on Lenamore. Lovely little grey horse. Only fifteen-two you know. Not as little as your Comet, of course. He's only fourteen-two – just a pony..."

Issie couldn't believe it! Tiggy simply would not shut up! The journalist was still blithering on in her ear and it was almost impossible for Issie to hear what Blaire was saying. She was certain that she'd just missed some vital piece of information about the equipment check before the horses went into the start box!

"...and that concludes our briefing," Blaire said, picking up her notes from the lectern. "I hope you're all ready for the kick-off on Friday. Thanks very much for coming – there will be coffee and cake served in the main foyer and you'll have a chance to talk to the press."

Issie watched in horror as Blaire left the stage.

"Don't worry," Avery whispered to Issie. "I made notes. I'll fill you in later…"

"You must be Tom Avery!" Tiggy leant over to introduce herself. "I'm Tiggy Brocklebent; so glad to meet you. I was just telling young Isadora that I'd love to write a feature on her for *Horsing Around* magazine."

"Ummm, Tiggy?" Issie said. "I'm really flattered that you want to do a story on me, but I don't think I'll be interesting enough. There are lots of other riders here who are far more experienced than me…"

"That's the point!" Tiggy said brightly. "I've written about all of them a hundred times before. They're all seasoned professionals, but not you! You're fresh – you're news!"

Tiggy pulled out her shorthand notebook and wielded her biro. "Now don't be shy. I want to know everything!"

Tiggy wasn't exaggerating. She kept Issie for nearly two hours, talking about her horses – not just Comet, but all of the horses she'd ridden over the years, plus the history behind the wild Blackthorn Ponies at her aunt's farm in Gisborne, and Francoise and Tom's new base at Laurel Farm in Wiltshire.

"Is it daunting to be riding in your first Four-Star?" Tiggy asked. "It must be strange being surrounded by famous faces? Have the other riders been welcoming to you?"

"It's pretty scary," Issie said. "But everyone has been really nice so far."

"Have you made any friends in the riders' village?" Tiggy asked.

"Well, I already knew Shane Campbell – we rode against each other when we were competing at the Young Rider Challenge in Australia," Issie explained. "And I met Marcus Pearce on the way here at a horse motel. He's riding for the Valmont Stables."

At the mention of the Valmont Stables Tiggy's demeanour suddenly changed completely.

"A terrible business, the death of Valmont Promise." Tiggy shook her head and then leant closer and whispered conspiratorially to Issie. "I was the journalist that covered the story, you know. So many unanswered questions! The vet's notes afterwards said he had a massive heart attack." Tiggy narrowed her eyes and whispered.

"Personally, I have my suspicions that drugs were involved."

Issie frowned. "What do you mean?"

"Let's just say I don't think he died of *natural* causes," Tiggy said. "I'd been at the three-day event in Pau watching him compete and Promise flew through the vet check beforehand. That horse had a perfectly healthy heart. And then the next thing you know, he's lying dead on the course! It doesn't take a genius to figure out that it just doesn't add up. The star of the Valmont Stables, a horse worth several million dollars, suddenly dies and no one can find the cause? It's all a bit fishy, if you ask me."

Tiggy suddenly pursed her lips. "You mustn't go around repeating any of this of course – I'd be liable for slander! But as far as I'm concerned there's more to the Promise story than anyone realises." She lowered her voice to a whisper once again. "All I will say is that a lot of people have a vendetta against Tyrel Valmont. He's a very unpopular man. I'm convinced that there are dirty dealings going on and a massive cover-up of the truth! If you ask me—"

But before Issie could, Avery had interrupted.

"I'm very sorry, Tiggy, but Issie really has to go now. We've got the showjumping arena booked for three p.m. and we can't be late."

As they said their goodbyes and headed back to Comet's stall, Issie wished Avery hadn't stopped Tiggy talking when he did.

"I thought you'd be glad to get away from that old gasbag!" Avery said.

"She was telling me about Valmont Promise," Issie said. "You know, the horse that had the heart attack on the cross-country course? Tiggy thinks there's more to it – like there was something sinister about the way Promise died."

Avery shook his head. "Heart attacks happen," he said, "especially when a horse is galloping. It puts their heart under extreme pressure – and the modern cross-country course is incredibly tough. Six kilometres at a flat gallop is enough to put a strain on even the most sound, healthy horse."

He looked at Issie's face. "I get the feeling that something else is bothering you too."

Issie hesitated. "It's… a big step up for me, isn't it? I never realised just how big the jumps would be here compared to a Three-Star course."

Avery nodded. "You know, back in my day when I rode at Badminton and Burghley, the three-day event was quite different. It was the same three basic phases, in the same order – dressage on the first day, followed by cross-country on day two and showjumping on the third day. But so much has changed in the modern three-day event – each phase is much harder than ever before. The dressage test you'll be performing on Friday is so complex with flying changes, half-passes and pirouettes, and on Saturday the cross-country phase is a six-kilometre gallop over thirty big fences. The horses will be stiff and sore, but they'll still have to pass the trot-up the next day before they're allowed on to the showjumping phase. The new scoring systems make it crucial to go clear because a single knocked pole is all it takes to lose the competition."

Avery paused and then added, "It's hard enough for the big horses, but even worse for Comet. He's a tiny pony facing up to massive jumps and having to compete against hacks that are twice his size."

"Err, Tom?" Issie pulled a face at him. "Pep talks have never been your strong point, but this has got to be one of the worst ever – totally depressing!"

"Issie, what do you want me to tell you? That riding in a Four-Star competition against the very best riders in the world will be easy? That there won't be moments on the cross-country course where you'll look at the sheer size of those fences and feel your stomach clench?"

Avery suddenly looked very serious. "I can't lie to you, Issie. The Kentucky Four-Star is a step up from anything you've ever done before. There are only six Four-Star courses in the world and Kentucky is one of them – this is as tough and as scary as it gets. This is one of the top international eventing competitions…"

Avery paused, "…and I really think you can win it."

"What?" Issie was shocked.

"Comet is ready for this," Avery said quietly, "and so are you, Issie. You're the youngest competitor here, but you have talent beyond your years. And I believe in your ability. So from the moment you step into that dressage arena on Friday, you keep your eye on the prize and don't you ever dare to doubt yourself. We're not here for the 'experience' or to make up the numbers. We're here because we're going to win."

Issie felt a rush of emotion overpower her. There was a lump in her throat and she had to choke it down before she could speak. "I take it back, Tom. Your pep talks are definitely improving."

Avery smiled. "Come on, we've got jumping practice to do."

Chapter 8

Avery might not have put much stock in anything that Tiggy Brocklebent had to say, but Stella lapped up the journalist's gossip. Back in the cabin that evening, she sat on the edge of the bed with wide eyes as Issie went through the whole conversation with Tiggy word for word.

"So Tiggy thinks someone hates Valmont enough to target his horses?" Stella asked. "Does she have any ideas who?"

"Not really," Issie said. "To be honest, Valmont seems like the sort of guy who would have a long list of enemies. I mean, you should have heard the way he talked to Marcus and Tara yesterday when he was checking up on Liberty. He virtually told Marcus that if he didn't win the Four-Star he'd lose his job."

"Ohmygod!" Stella's eyes went wide. "Issie! You don't think that Marcus has a grudge against Valmont, do you?"

"Stella, what are you talking about?" Issie replied. "Of course not! That's crazy!"

"No, it's not," Stella said. "Think about it. Marcus has every reason to hate his boss if he's so horrible to him. Marcus knew Promise – and he was working for the Valmont Stables when Promise died. Plus he was also there that night in the motel stables at Rio Rancho! I mean, nobody else was around, were they? Maybe *he* was trying to hurt Liberty to get back at Valmont and you got in the way! How do you know that it wasn't Marcus lurking in the shadows in the first place? You disturbed him in the act and then he pretended that he was coming to help!"

"Marcus isn't capable of harming a horse," Issie said. "And he wouldn't intentionally hurt the horse that he's supposed to be riding."

"How do you know that?" Stella said. "You only met him a week ago. He could be a totally bonkers horse killer! Just because he's crazy about you, doesn't mean he can't also just be crazy full-stop."

"Stella!" Issie snapped. "I keep telling you – there's nothing going on with me and Marcus…"

She was interrupted by a knock on their cabin door. Before she had the chance to answer, the handle turned and the door swung open. It was Marcus Pearce.

"Hi," he smiled at them. "What's going on? A private team meeting?"

"Ummm, sort of," Issie said nervously. Had Marcus heard their conversation? Was he listening outside their door? If he did know what they had been talking about then he certainly wasn't letting on.

"I just came to ask you both to a party tonight," Marcus said. "Gerhardt Muller is throwing a bash over at his horse truck."

"Uhhh, thanks, but we really shouldn't go out tonight," Issie said. "We've got the trotting-up tomorrow and—"

"We'd love to come!" Stella interrupted her. "What time?"

"The party's at eight. Meet you there?" Marcus said.

"Cool!" Stella said. "See you then."

"I can't believe you talked me into this," Issie said as the girls cut through the stable blocks to get to Gerhardt's truck. "I should be back at home studying my dressage test."

"Issie," Stella said, "you've been studying that test for so long you could ride it with your eyes shut. What's wrong with taking one night off and having fun?"

Fun wasn't exactly high on Issie's list of priorities. Last night she had lain awake in bed at three in the morning worrying about Laurel Farm and the future. If she lost at Kentucky, they would have to sell another horse to make ends meet. And even though Avery and Francoise hadn't actually come out and said as much, she knew that it would probably be Nightstorm. Issie's bay stallion was worth the most money by far, and his sale would be enough to keep the farm running for another few months.

Issie couldn't bear even considering the idea of selling her beloved Storm. He was Blaze's son and Issie had been there at the mare's side when he was born. She had watched him grow up into the amazing horse that he was today. At times during this journey she had regretted not bringing him with her to Kentucky instead of Comet. It wasn't an easy decision, choosing which horse to bring. She had discussed it at length with Francoise and Avery and in the end they had all agreed that Comet was the best choice for Kentucky. The little pony was better at travelling long distances than Storm was, and besides, Issie needed to save the big bay for the Badminton Horse Trials happening in just two weeks' time back in England. With the two events scheduled so close together there was no way she could ride Nightstorm at both.

This was the sort of decision professional eventers were forced to make – deciding to split their best horses over the various events on the calendar. But with their funds so low and things looking grim for the future, Issie was beginning to think she'd made the wrong call saving Nightstorm for Badminton. Was she asking too much of Comet to make it round this massive course at Lexington?

"Issie, you need to stop over-thinking things," Stella said gently. "Forget about horses – just for one night. I don't only want us to go because I want to see Shane. This party will be good for you too."

Issie wasn't so sure. "I'm not staying late," she warned Stella. "I'll talk to Marcus for a bit and then I'm going home."

The party was in full swing when they arrived. Most of the guests were crammed inside the tiny interior of Gerhardt's horse truck. The truck was one of those posh ones that was kitted out like a luxury yacht on wheels – with plush sofas and a state-of-the-art kitchen and living room upfront, and sleek horse stalls at the back. There were about twenty riders crammed into the space, talking and dancing.

"There's Shane!" Stella gave a quick wave and he pushed his way towards them through the crowd. The music was really loud and Issie found herself having to shout to be heard above the noise. "Have you seen Marcus?" she asked.

Shane shook his head. "He'll turn up soon."

"Come on!" Stella shouted to Issie and Shane. "I love this song! Let's dance!"

There wasn't much room in the cramped horse truck

so their dance moves involved mostly bouncing up and down. After crashing into at least three people Issie gave up. It was nearly nine now and Marcus still hadn't turned up. And even if he did, how was she supposed to talk to him over the pounding of the music? If she went back to her cabin she'd still have time to read through her dressage test a couple of times before bed. "Stella!" she shouted. "I'm going to go back to the cabin, OK?"

Stella nodded. "OK! See you there."

It was a relief to step outside the noisy horse truck into the cool night air. Issie jumped down the truck steps and headed back the way they had come, walking through the stable blocks, towards the riders' village.

At night the main lights in the loose boxes were switched off so that the horses were left in darkness, but in the corridors there were security lights offering just enough illumination so that Issie could find her way quite easily through the rows of stabling.

She had just entered stable block D, when she noticed a figure up ahead of her. In the gloom she couldn't make out who it was, but she could see straight away that they were acting very strangely – crouching down behind the feed bins and then creeping along beside the loose boxes.

Suddenly the figure stood up in the light in full view and turned round so that Issie could see his face.

It was Marcus!

Why was he in the stables at night, acting so weird? Issie was about to call out when Marcus suddenly leapt forward like a sprinter from the starting blocks and took off down the corridor away from her.

"Marcus?" Issie shouted after him. *What was going on?*

And then Issie realised why Marcus was running. There was someone else in the stables, a hooded figure that had slunk out of one of the stalls. Startled by the sight of Marcus bearing down on him, the hooded figure took off, sprinting out the door of the stable block.

Marcus kept running, following him outside into the yards and Issie tried to keep up.

As she came out of the doors of the stable block she was just in time to witness the hooded man reach out and snatch up a rake that was leaning against the wall. Then he turned and flung the rake at Marcus!

Thankfully Marcus had lightning reflexes. He managed

to duck in time, the rake missing him by less than a centimetre as it flew over his head, and then he was up and running again. He was faster than the hooded man and stride by stride he was gaining on him.

Suddenly the man veered sharply to the left, hurdling a post-and-rail fence. Marcus followed, but just as he was at the top of his arc over the fence, his foot hooked on the top rail.

With his foot caught on the rail Marcus was unable to regain his balance and he went down hard. He put his hands out to break the fall, but the surface beneath him was concrete and the impact was bone-crunching. He let out a cry as he hit the ground.

"Marcus!" Within moments she was by his side, leaning down over him. "Are you OK?"

Marcus looked up at her, his face racked with pain. "Uhhh… my arm, I think I've hurt it," he said.

Still bent over him, Issie noticed something lying on the concrete. A green security passcard – Marcus must have dropped it when he fell. She reached down, grasped it and shoved it in her pocket. "Stay still," she told him. "Don't move. I'll get help. It's going to be OK…"

Two hours later Issie found herself with Avery and Tara in the orthopaedic ward of Lexington General Hospital, watching as Marcus, his face drained pale from the shock and pain, sat stoically while the surgeon examined him.

When the doctor broke the news that the bone was broken – and not just in one place but in two – Marcus completely lost it. "It can't be broken. I'm due to compete in the Kentucky Four-Star on Friday. I have to ride."

"Very funny," the doctor said drily. "It will be at least four weeks before you can get on a horse again."

"But that's impossible!" Marcus tried to stand up. "Look, let's just leave it for now and I'll ride with it like this. I'll come back when the competition is over and you can put a cast on it then."

"Sit down, son," the doctor said, his patience clearly strained to breaking point. "Your arm is badly broken. If you try and use it you'll end up with permanent nerve damage. We need to immobilise the bones immediately – please, let us give you a sedative so we can reset the bone and put on the plaster cast."

In the end, Marcus had to admit defeat and let them encase his arm in plaster from his elbow to his fingertips. He still refused the sedative.

"I don't want to sleep," he insisted. "I need to tell you guys what happened. There was a man, I saw him going into Liberty's stall… arghhh!" Marcus winced with pain as the surgeon repositioned his arm. "Tara, you need to get back to the stables – someone has to be there to keep an eye on Liberty. Something is definitely going on – she's not safe."

"Calm down," Tara reassured him, "I'll go to the stables now and keep a watch on her, OK?"

Tara turned to Avery and Issie. "Can you stay with Marcus until the doctor is finished and then bring him back to the Horsepark?"

"Of course," Avery said.

As the doctor finished plastering the cast, Issie tried to take Marcus's mind off the pain, by telling him stories about Comet.

"Back at my aunt's farm he was always in trouble,"

Issie said. "He was constantly jumping out of his paddock. The first time I met him we nearly hit him with a horse truck because he'd managed to get on to the driveway. And then there was the time he jumped out and got into the tack shed and ate all the dog biscuits."

"I've never heard of a horse eating dog biscuits before," Marcus said, momentarily distracted from the pain. "Aren't horses supposed to be vegetarians?"

"Tell that to Comet!" Issie smiled. "He once stole a meat pie off the back of the horse truck while I was trying to plait his mane!"

Marcus laughed – and then instantly regretted it. "Oww! Don't make me laugh," he said. "It hurts."

"Sorry," Issie said. "Hey, by the way," she passed him the green passcard, "I picked up your security card when you fell. You must have dropped it."

Marcus shook his head. "No, I've still got my card." He produced it from his pocket. "That isn't mine."

Issie stared at the green passcard in her hand, and then put it back in her pocket. The doctor was now giving the cast a final wipe with a damp cloth. "You're all done, Marcus. You're free to leave."

"I'll go and get the car and bring it round to the door," Avery said to Issie. "You bring him down in the lift and I'll meet you out front."

As Avery left the room, Issie gathered up Marcus's things ready to leave and turned to him. "OK, let's go," she said. But Marcus wasn't moving. He was sitting on the side of the bed with a serious expression on his face.

"Issie," he said. "Wait. Can I talk to you for a moment?"

"Yeah, of course," Issie said. "What is it?"

Marcus held up his newly plastered broken arm. "You may have noticed that I've got a little problem," he said darkly. "It looks like I'm not going to be able to ride in the Four-Star."

Issie didn't know what to say. "There'll be other years…"

"No. There won't be," Marcus replied. "This was my big chance. I'd been training that mare for six months. Mr Valmont was counting on me to bring Liberty home in the top ten – if I can't ride her, he'll dump me. I'll lose my contract."

"But it was an accident," Issie said. "You were trying to protect Liberty. I'm sure he'll understand…"

"You've met Valmont," Marcus said. "Did he seem

like an understanding kind of guy to you? The only way to keep him happy is to find another rider to take over the ride on Liberty."

"You're kidding!" Issie said. "How are you going to find someone at the last minute who…" And then she saw the expectant look on his face.

"Ohmygod, Marcus, no! I couldn't!"

"Issie, please, it's the only way."

Marcus looked up at her with pleading eyes and she knew that he wasn't joking. "Issie, I want you to compete in my place. I'm asking you to take over the ride on Valmont Liberty."

Chapter 9

When Issie was a junior rider at Chevalier Point Pony Club she never thought that one day she'd be given the chance to ride a mare like Valmont Liberty. It was the kind of offer that every pony-club kid dreamt of. Which made it all the harder to say no.

"I'm sorry, Marcus," Issie said. "I can't do it – not like this."

"Why not?" Marcus said. "You're already registered to compete and so is Liberty – I'm sure Blaire can swap over the paperwork. You won't be breaking any rules. There'll be loads of other riders entering on more than one horse."

"Marcus!" Issie was stunned. "Those riders have all had months to build a relationship with their horses. You want me to do it with Liberty in one day! We've only got tomorrow before the dressage test."

"I can help you," Marcus insisted. "I know how Liberty thinks. I can coach you, teach you how to handle her."

"The whole idea is mad. I just can't do it. I've got to focus on Comet – I can't afford to be distracted."

Marcus looked devastated. "I know it's a lot to ask, Issie. I know we've only just met really and you don't owe me anything, but please. If you could just get her round the cross-country and put in a half-decent showjumping round, maybe it would be enough to save my job."

Issie groaned and then slumped down on to the hospital bed to sit beside him.

"Let me talk to Tom and see what he says," she said eventually. "But I'm not promising anything."

Marcus looked incredibly relieved. "Fantastic! Thanks, Issie."

"Don't thank me yet!" Issie said. "I know what Tom's

like. He's going to think that this is a crazy plan. He won't allow anything to interfere with my schedule on Comet. I bet he says no way."

"I think you should do it."

"Excuse me?" Issie couldn't believe it. They had dropped Marcus back at his cabin and then she told Avery about the offer of the chance ride. She'd expected him to dismiss the idea outright, but instead, Tom was actually agreeing with Marcus's plan!

"It's a great opportunity," Avery said. "Riding a horse the calibre of Liberty round the course at Kentucky would be great experience for you."

"But Tom!" Issie said. "I've only got one day – how am I supposed to bond with Liberty in that time?"

"I'm not expecting you to understand this mare deeply in twenty-four hours," Avery admitted, "but you're a good enough rider now to get on just about any horse and know which buttons to push to get them round a course. Remember the year that Mark Todd rode Badminton on Horton Point, a horse he'd only just swung a leg over the day before? He didn't have more than a day to get to know that horse and he won it, Issie!"

"But what about Comet? I've already got a horse to ride."

"Mark Todd rode two horses round Badminton that year," Avery countered. "And what about British rider Lorna Clarke? She rode three different horses round Badminton in one day."

Issie sighed. "I do want to ride her, Tom. Liberty is a great horse…"

"So what's holding you back?" Avery asked.

"I just don't want to let everyone down," Issie said. "I mean, we've packed up our lives and moved to Laurel Farm for this, and everything is riding on me making it into the top ten with Comet – and now Marcus needs me to bring Liberty home as well! It's too much pressure!"

"Issie," Avery was serious, "a professional rider is always under pressure. When you came to me years ago and asked me to be your trainer I told you that it would be like this, that you would need to be tough – physically and mentally – to cope with this career. As a rider at elite level you go out on that cross-country course carrying the hopes and dreams of your team, your fans and your nation on your shoulders. I know how terrifying that is because I've done it myself. But here you are with this brilliant opportunity, this chance ride, and you're letting your fears get in the way."

"I'm not afraid," Issie shot back.

"Then stop hesitating," Avery said. "Issie, this is what you've been trained to do."

Issie groaned. "I'm not going to win this fight, am I?"

Avery shook his head. "You might as well give in now and save yourself the bother."

Issie was silent for a long time and then finally she turned to her trainer. "OK then. I'll do it," she said. Then she added, "But you have to be the one to break the news to Stella. She's going to have a blue fit when she finds out that she's got two horses to groom for me."

Avery smiled. "That's my girl! Let's go tell Marcus the good news."

After the trip to hospital it was past midnight when Issie finally got to bed, but she still set the alarm for 5 a.m. Thursday was going to be a big day.

Her first morning task was a second walk-through of the cross-country course. Marcus wasn't really capable of walking around with his newly broken arm, Stella was grooming both horses in preparation for the trotting-up and Tara and Avery were sorting out Issie and Liberty's paperwork with Blaire Andrews, so Issie walked it alone.

She'd been hoping that the cross-country course would be less terrifying this time around, and certainly some fences appeared less daunting. But as she stood on the precipice of the deep, deep ditch in front of the Gamekeeper's Brush she felt completely and utterly sick. If there had been any other alternative she would gladly have taken it, but the Gamekeeper's Brush offered no choice – there was just one way to go. *Actually*, Issie thought as she looked at the jump, *there are two ways to go – over the fence or down into the ditch!*

Unable to shake off her feeling of dread, she moved on to fence 25, the Tobacco Stripping Table – a flat rustic tabletop. She was confident about this jump. It was very wide, but Comet would clear it easily, and his little stridings would come in useful at the next fence too – the Normandy Bank, which required the horses to leap up on to a grassy mound then take a stride, jump a trakehner at the top of the bank and then jump back down again off the other side of the bank.

As she paced out the stridings, she was trying to imagine jumping the same bank on Liberty. The mare was so physically different to Comet. Her strides would be much bigger.

By the time she arrived back at the stables Issie was even more nervous than she had been last night. At least with Comet, she understood how his mind worked, all his little quirks and his foibles. Like the way he sometimes stood back from a fence and she needed to keep her legs on right until the last moment, or his tendency to veer to the right if he was planning to run out. But with Liberty she didn't have a clue what the mare would do. The horse was a total mystery to her – and she was about to ride her round one of the biggest cross-country courses in the world! Maybe there was still a chance to back out of this.

"The paperwork is all sorted," Avery announced when Issie arrived at the stables. "Blaire has given the rider transfer her stamp of approval."

"I've spoken to Mr Valmont too," Tara told Issie. "He's agreed to let you take over the ride and he's planning to come and watch your dressage test tomorrow."

"Great," Issie said. "Really… that's… great."

Avery looked at his watch. "We've got the trotting-up in half an hour. You'll need to trot both horses for the judges and then you can give Comet his final workout." Avery turned to Tara. "Issie should be free by two – we can meet you here again then and she can ride Liberty."

"Excellent," Tara agreed. "I'll have the mare ready for you."

The trotting-up was a glamorous event – a bit like the celebrity red-carpet walk before a film premiere. The horses would always be presented perfectly groomed with plaited manes and the riders would dress up in their best outfits. A crowd would gather to watch the horses trot as the judges checked them to see if they were sound and ready to compete.

For her outfit that day Issie had chosen a simple black skirt and a cream blouse, and a pair of flat, black brogues.

"Boring!" Stella had pronounced as she watched Issie getting dressed. She dug around in her own suitcase and pulled out the dress she'd worn to the party the night before, a brightly patterned violet and blue sundress with frills on the edge. "Why don't you borrow this?"

"I'm not trying to scare the horses," Issie responded.

"It's pretty," Stella said.

"I don't want to look pretty," Issie replied, "I want to look professional."

"You look like a professional bore. At least wear your floral shirt instead of that cream one!"

Issie sighed. "All right! But I don't see what the fuss is about anyway. Everyone will be looking at the horses, they won't be looking at me."

She was wrong about that. The crowd that had gathered for the trotting-up gave Issie the loudest round of applause when she stepped forward, leading Comet alongside her in his bridle to take her turn.

And when she took the reins with Liberty and trotted the mare back and forth to the approval of the judges, who passed both her horses as fit and healthy, the crowd went wild.

"I don't understand it." Issie was bewildered and in a daze when she arrived back at the cabin with Stella. "There were loads of famous riders there. How did the crowd even know who I am?"

It turned out that the reason was Tiggy Brocklebent. The writer from *Horsing Around* magazine had been blogging about Issie on her website.

"Tiggy has half a million readers," Stella said excitedly, "and she's written a whole column about you. Listen to this…"

Stella began to read Tiggy's blog aloud to Issie: "*She's the youngest rider ever to compete here at Kentucky – and not content with trying to get a fourteen-two pony round one of the world's toughest courses, this determined seventeen-year-old girl has now taken on an even greater challenge – a chance ride. Filling in for the injured Marcus Pearce, Isadora Brown will now be riding the Valmont Stables' star performer, Valmont Liberty, as her second mount here in Kentucky. Can this teenage girl change the course of eventing history? Keep reading my blog to find out!*"

"Ohmygod!" Issie groaned. "That's all I need…"

There was a knock on the door of their cabin and Avery stuck his head round the corner. "Come on," he said, "Comet is waiting for his workout."

After Issie had put Comet through his paces and Stella had tacked Liberty up in her dressage saddle, Issie got some last-minute words of advice from Marcus.

"Liberty is the most sensitive horse I've ever ridden," he told Issie. "You have to ride her really quietly in the dressage arena because she's prone to, well, explode."

"Explode?" Issie squeaked, "What do you mean 'explode'?"

Marcus winced at the question. "The last time I was competing her she got a bit upset when we were doing the flying changes through the middle of the arena and she had a bucking fit."

Issie's eyes went wide. "You didn't tell me any of this before!"

"I didn't think it was a big deal!" Marcus said. "It wasn't really a fit – it was only three or four bucks. It's not like she was trying to throw me off or anything

– she was just a bit excited. And we managed to finish the test after that. I'm sure she won't do it again."

He had finished adjusting the stirrups and stepped back. "There! All done. Shall we head over to the arena?"

Avery and Tara came over with them to watch, but it was Marcus who took control of the first half of the training session. He was the one who had been riding Liberty for the past six months and he knew the mare best.

"She's better on the left rein, so ride that way first to warm up," Marcus told Issie. Issie began to ride Liberty around the arena, walking her at first and then trotting and cantering. The mare's paces were huge and ground-covering compared to tiny Comet and her trot was so floaty and elevated that it took Issie a moment to get into the groove.

"Don't ride her too much," Marcus called out. "Sit really quiet on her. All you need to do is make the slightest move and she'll—"

He didn't get the chance to finish his sentence because Issie, who was trying to get Liberty to canter, had put her legs in the wrong spot and felt the mare go into a huge extended trot down the side of the arena.

"Oops!" Issie said as she brought her back to a walk, "Pressed the wrong buttons!"

Half an hour later, Issie had finally refined her cues and she was feeling much better. The mare was super-tuned and so sensitive that if you put your leg too far forward or back, or shifted your weight to the wrong spot, you could end up doing a piaffe or a pirouette when all you wanted was a basic trot. But Issie felt confident that she had the hang of it now.

"You've got her well trained," she told Marcus as they stood and waited for Stella to swap the mare into her cross-country saddle.

They weren't allowed to practise the cross-country jumps on the actual course today, but there were several other cross-country jumps available for the riders to train over around the Kentucky Horsepark grounds. They walked the mare to a small group of rustic fences that were set up beside the showjumping arena. There was a massive wooden dog kennel, a trakehner and a substantial ditch and hedge combination a bit like a miniature version of the Gamekeeper's Brush.

"Liberty is inclined to rush her fences and can get away on me sometimes," Marcus admitted. "I tend to school her at a steady canter rather than let her gallop on too much."

Issie nodded and then stood up in her stirrups in two-point position and began to canter the mare around, getting her into a rhythm, becoming accustomed to her extravagant movement. Liberty seemed calm enough, but as soon as she caught sight of the first fence it was a different story. She took the dog kennel at a fast canter, leaning on Issie's hands and then by the time she reached the trakehner she was in a flat gallop. Issie sat right back and hauled on the reins to try and pull her up, but Liberty wasn't having it. She flew the trakehner without slowing down and she was still galloping when the ditch and hedge came into view.

"Steady, girl," Issie said firmly, giving the reins a quick tug in the hope of alerting Liberty to the fact that she was the one in charge here. But Liberty ignored Issie's tugs. In fact it didn't make a blind bit of difference what Issie did. Liberty had no intention of slowing down. She came at the jump in a gallop, barrelling at top speed at the fence. And then, when she was just three strides out from the jump, Liberty suddenly spied the ditch.

"Don't look down into the ditch!" Marcus called out to Issie. "Drive her on with your legs and look up!"

But it was too late. Issie's eyes were drawn down and so were Liberty's. They both stared into the chasm in front of the hedge and Liberty sensed her rider's hesitation and stopped galloping. She skidded to a stop so suddenly that, despite being in the classic eventing rider's safety position, Issie was flung forward with such force that she was catapulted out of the saddle.

Issie flipped in a complete somersault through the air, and then she was coming down, bracing for the unavoidable impact as the ditch rushed up to meet her and she fell into the void below.

Chapter 10

Twenty thousand spectators had gathered in the grand-stands of the main arena at the Kentucky Horsepark to watch the first, crucial phase of the Three-Day Event. Already that morning, the crowd had watched as fifty-three of the world's greatest eventers performed their dressage tests. Now, the crowd was hushed in tense silence as a teenage girl on a 14.2 skewbald pony warmed up around the dressage arena and prepared for her moment in front of the judges.

"This is the one we've all been waiting for." The crisp, British voice of the announcer, Mike Partridge, crackled back to life over the Tannoy.

"It certainly is, Mike," his co-announcer, the famous

American former showjumping star Betsy Bevan agreed. "We're about to see the young rider who's got everyone talking here in Lexington."

"She's only seventeen," Mike Partridge continued, "so what an experience to be competing here at the famed Kentucky Horsepark. Making her Four-Star eventing debut, ladies and gentlemen, this is Isadora Brown riding Blackthorn Comet."

As she took her last warm-up lap round the edge of the dressage arena Issie tried to ignore the announcers and the buzz of the crowd. The last thing she needed right now was to get anxious and lose the plot. This morning she'd sat on the sidelines and watched some of her heroes perform, the superstars of the eventing world. She'd been in awe of Gerhardt Muller and his black stallion, Avatar, who had performed one of the most brilliant dressage tests she'd ever seen. And now, here she was, a kid from Chevalier Point Pony Club. What made her think she could foot it with these Four-Star professionals?

But if Issie had doubts, Comet never questioned their right to be here. He was a star and he knew it. As they trotted round the arena, Comet snorted and strutted, eager and ready to perform, and Issie suddenly knew in her bones that this was going to be one of his good days.

Dressage was always the hardest phase for the little skewbald, but Francoise and Issie had worked hard together over the past few months at Laurel Farm, improving his education, and Comet was now incredibly well schooled. He still didn't like dressage much, but Issie knew that today she had a secret weapon on her side. If there was one thing that Comet loved, it was performing in front of a crowd. When he entered the arena and saw twenty-thousand pairs of eyes watching him from the stands it was like an electric current had run through him. Suddenly he was super-charged. Every muscle in his body was quivering, his neck was beautifully arched and his tail lifted like an Arabian's so that it flowed out behind him. As far as Comet was concerned he was no longer an ill-bred wild pony from the hill country of Gisborne, he was a fabulous, international dressage schoolmaster!

Now it was up to Issie to keep the little skewbald under control and stop his high spirits from going over the top, while giving him all the right cues to complete his test.

As she entered at A and cantered up the centre line she felt her heart racing as she saw the judge staring back at her. She pulled Comet to a brilliant square halt at X to salute, the judge raised her hand back, and then, it began.

Issie had run through this test so many times in her mind, she knew every single movement off by heart. There was the working trot to begin with, and then the extended trot down the long side of the arena. Comet flung his forelegs out in front of him as if he were flying. His nostrils flared and his veins bulged as he put everything he had into every stride.

"Look at this pony move!" Mike Partridge enthused in reverent tones to the crowd. "That was a perfect extended trot, and now we see Isadora performing the one-time flying changes across the arena."

"That's right, Mike," Betsy Bevan joined in the commentary. "The horse must keep the rhythm and change canter leads with every single stride. This is a true test of control."

"Magnificent one-time changes!" Mike Partridge

raved. "And we're back into the canter – and the pirouettes down the centre line. This pony hasn't put a hoof wrong! And there we have it, the half-pass in trot across the diagonal and up the centre line for the final salute."

"It was a great test, Mike," Betsy Bevan said. "For a first-time effort she has to be happy with that."

"I'm no judge by any means, Betsy," Mike added, "but I'm betting that this puts her in the top ten – what a fabulous effort!"

As Issie and Comet rode out of the arena the crowd erupted in applause. It had been a fantastic dressage test, the best that Comet had ever done, and Issie looked thrilled to bits as Avery and Stella met her in the collection ring at the far side of the grandstands.

"Brilliant! Brilliant! Brilliant!" Avery gave her a round of applause.

"Comet, you are such a star!" Stella took the skewbald's reins. "You are totally getting extra barley in your hard feed tonight!"

"Oh man, I am exhausted after that!" Issie took off her silk top hat and slid down out of the saddle. She gave a grunt of pain as her feet hit the ground. Her face suddenly turned pale and she made a grab at her ribs.

"Are you OK?" Avery asked.

"I'm fine," Issie said unconvincingly.

What nobody in the crowded stands at the Kentucky Horsepark realised was that underneath her dressage jacket Issie was bruised the colour of an aubergine.

When she had fallen into the ditch yesterday her protective cross-country air jacket had inflated instantly on impact and puffed up round her torso like the airbags of a car. It had prevented her spine from suffering serious injury, but it still hadn't been enough to cushion her completely.

Issie had insisted to Avery and Tara that she was OK, although the truth was that she suspected one of her ribs might be cracked. But what was the point in mentioning it? There was no treatment apart from a few bandages for cracked ribs. The bones would eventually heal themselves. She had told Stella about it – well, actually Stella had caught sight of the bruises when they were getting ready for bed last night, so she had no choice. But Issie made her friend promise not to tell Avery. He would only worry about her – he might even make her withdraw from the competition and there was no way she was doing that.

The fall had been a bad moment in the training session on Liberty. Avery, however, had been insistent that Issie's failure to get the mare over the jump wasn't a portent of doom. "It's always strange schooling a horse over cross-country fences in cold blood. It's a totally different story to riding the real thing," he said, reassuring her. "When your blood is up and Liberty is feeling psyched then the extra adrenalin will kick in and that will change everything."

There was no point in worrying about the cross-country now – she had to get Liberty through the dressage phase first. The mare was due to perform in the arena in an hour. Issie would have to get onboard soon and begin warming up for her test.

"How are you feeling?" Stella asked as she came to take Comet back to his stall.

"I'm good," Issie said.

"No, really," Stella looked concerned. "Do your ribs hurt?"

"Only when I breathe or move," Issie replied.

"Maybe you should tell Avery," Stella said. "It's too much riding both of them in your condition."

"No," Issie shook her head, "I can't quit, I promised Marcus I'd ride her. It's too late to back out now."

In the practice arena Issie let Liberty have a long rein at first, encouraging the mare to stretch her neck and relax. She was the opposite of Comet and needed to be treated so differently to get the best out of her. Issie was able to gather Comet up almost straight away into a trot when she was warming him up, but with Liberty she kept the mare in a walk for ages, talking to her softly as she rode, trying to calm and relax her before finally shortening up the reins ready to trot.

It was a painfully slow way to warm up, but it worked. By the time Issie asked Liberty to trot on, the mare was no longer acting like she was walking on hot coals. As Issie collected her up and began to do the more advanced manoeuvres, Liberty responded beautifully. Marcus was right, she was an extremely sensitive and schooled mare. The problem was that she was almost too well schooled and if you put one foot or hand in the wrong place Liberty might misread your instructions and suddenly you'd be doing a pirouette!

Avery watched as Issie worked the horse in, offering the odd comment to help out. Then, when the moment of truth drew near, he headed over to Issie and gestured at the clock above the warm-up arena.

"Time to go," he said. "You're due in the main arena."

Issie nodded. "We're ready, Tom."

As Issie rode Liberty towards the main arena, with Avery striding along at their side, Stella came running up to them.

"Comet's dressage scores have been posted!" Stella panted. "Issie, you got thirty-six!"

Issie was gobsmacked. Thirty-six was the best score she'd ever had in her life! In three-day eventing the scoring system worked backwards, which meant that the lowest dressage score was the winning score, and thirty-six was super-low. It might even put her in the top ten!

"I just thought you'd like to know before you went back in there with Liberty," Stella beamed up at her. "Good luck!"

The news of Comet's amazing score was just the confidence booster that Issie needed. As she headed back into the main arena to complete her second dressage test of the day she suddenly found herself sitting up a little bit straighter and prouder in the saddle. She had aced this once – now all she had to do was make the right moves once again on Liberty.

"She's back, ladies and gentlemen," Mike Partridge announced gaily over the Tannoy. "You've already seen this young girl put in a fabulous test on The Pony. Now here she is, on a chance ride that she only got handed yesterday, this amazing silver dapple mare from the Valmont Stables in California. This is Isadora Brown, back in the arena once more on Valmont Liberty!"

As she cantered up the centre line, Issie knew she was on a hair trigger with this horse. Riding Liberty was like being perched on a volcano and any little thing might set her off. Issie had to handle her absolutely perfectly or it would be a disaster.

As she made her salute for the second time that day, the crowd was hushed and reverent, saving their applause until she finished the test so that they wouldn't upset the horse. Even Mike Partridge seemed to understand that this mare was a potential time bomb, and was whispering his comments over the loudspeaker.

"A magnificent entrance," he said. "A lovely extended trot, and look at those paces!"

As Issie trotted up the far side of the arena she was completely focused on keeping Liberty in a perfect extended trot. The mare was round and supple, they were a perfect team. And then suddenly it all fell apart.

This was a world-class, Four-Star event so there were cameramen positioned at the far end of the arena filming the competitors with a massive camera mounted on a tall mobile crane. Liberty hadn't noticed the cameramen before, but as the crane began to move, the mare suddenly spotted it and gave a massive spook! She bounded sideways into the middle of the arena and it took all of Issie's skill, strength and determination to force the quivering, terrified Liberty back to where she was supposed to be.

"Bad luck!" Betsy Bevan commiserated from the announcers' booth. "Liberty has shied at the TV cameras. Let's hope this untested combination can remain on track for the rest of the dressage test."

In the arena, Issie was trying to refocus. She'd completely blown her points on that particular manoeuvre – but a dressage test was always judged as a series of separate movements. Just because the mare had wigged out for one movement didn't mean they couldn't still pull themselves together and continue on to get a good score. Issie had to keep Liberty calm. They had reached the next marker now and Issie had regained her composure. She confidently asked the mare to move into her one-time canter changes and Liberty responded on cue, doing the movements perfectly.

There was a moment when they came up the centre line once more to perform the pirouettes and Liberty once again saw the TV cameras ahead of her. Issie sensed the mare's apprehension and spoke softly to reassure Liberty that the camera wasn't going to eat her. The mare seemed to understand. She didn't spook as they rode past the camera this time. After that, the rest of the test was a breeze. Issie continued to ride the silver dapple mare so pitch-perfectly that Liberty never had a reason to go wrong. As they came back up the centre line one final time for their salute to the judges the crowd held their breath, breaking into deafening applause as Issie and Liberty left the ring.

"Disaster at first, but what a remarkable recovery!" Mike Partridge enthused. "What a crowd favourite this seventeen-year-old girl is proving to be!"

Issie had never been so relieved to finish a test! As she rode out of the main arena she saw Tara and Marcus waiting for her in the wings with smiles on their faces.

"I'm really sorry," Issie said as she joined them. "I never even considered that she might shy at the cameras."

"There was nothing you could have done about it," Tara reassured her. "The great thing is that you didn't lose your cool when it happened and you finished with a great test!"

"Miss Brown!"

Issie looked up and saw Tyrel Valmont walking briskly towards her.

"Good work," Valmont said. "Unfortunate camera incident, but you rode the mare well."

"Thank you, Mr Valmont," Issie didn't know what to say. "It's down to Marcus really. He's got Liberty so well schooled that all I had to do was press the right buttons."

"I wouldn't be too hasty to give someone else the credit," Valmont said gruffly. "It was good riding on your part. I'm sure you'll give it everything you've got on the cross-country course tomorrow."

He looked over at Marcus who had taken Liberty's reins and was about to lead the mare back to her box.

"You can't handle her with your arm in a cast. Here – I'll take her back to the stall," he said grumpily, taking Liberty from Marcus.

Valmont headed off, leading Liberty towards the stables, but he had only gone a little way when he stopped abruptly and began to search his pockets.

"Lost something, sir?" Marcus asked.

"I don't seem to have my passcard for the stall on me," Valmont said. "I must have misplaced it…" He patted the pockets of his suit jacket.

Marcus dug into his jeans pocket and handed over

his own green card. "Here," he said. "You can take mine."

Issie couldn't help remembering the green passcard she had found on the ground that night when the intruder got away. Had Valmont dropped his card in the dark that night? But why would he be lurking around his own horse?

It didn't make sense. *Mind you*, Issie thought, *a lot of things about Valmont didn't make sense. OK, Marcus was injured, but since when did the super-rich head of the stables take it upon himself to volunteer to do a groom's job and put the horse away in its box?*

As she watched Valmont lead Liberty away, she heard her name being called. She turned round and saw Tom Avery hurrying over to join them. He had the strangest look on his face.

"Tom, what is it? Is something wrong?"

"Issie," Avery said. "The officials have just posted the final list of scores for the dressage test…"

"Ohmygod!" Issie bit her lip. "Tom? Where am I?"

"Issie, it's brilliant," Avery said. "Liberty is in eighth place and Comet is fifth!"

And for the first time ever that Issie could remember,

Avery lunged forward and gave her a hug. She felt a shock of pain in her ribs, but she didn't care because this was one of the best moments in her life.

"Issie, you've got two horses in the top ten!"

Chapter 11

Yesterday a plaited and polished Comet had trotted majestically into the arena to perform his dressage test. But today the dainty plaits and elegant dressage saddle were gone. Comet was kitted out in serious cross-country equipment, the full battle armour of martingale, breastplate and grackle noseband with sets of leather tendon boots front and back to protect him from impact as well as a set of white bell boots up front.

The change in costume hadn't gone unnoticed by the little skewbald. He knew exactly why he was dressed this way and his eyes were shining with anticipation. Cross-country was the phase of three-day eventing that he truly loved and he couldn't wait to get on the course.

In the loose box with him, Issie was also dressed in protective body armour. She wore a high-impact helmet, gloves and her air-tech jacket was rigged so that a fall would set it off instantly. She checked the jacket panels and did up the zips on her leather riding boots while Stella continued to work away on Comet's legs, applying a thick layer of white grease to the front of his legs, smothering the stifle and knees. The grease was used to help the horse to slide over a fence if he caught it with his legs, and hopefully the slippery substance would also offer a coating of protection to keep him from getting cuts and scrapes on the course.

Stella stood back and admired her work. The white paste made it look like the skewbald had even more white patches than before. "He's ready for you," she said.

"Just a second," Issie replied. She had strapped on her stopwatch and was now doing up the tabs on her competition number, which she wore over the air-tech vest.

"It's crazy, isn't it?" Stella said as she handed Issie the reins. "You and me getting ready to ride the Four-Star. I never believed this would really happen."

"I know," Issie agreed. "It seems like just yesterday that we were little kids together at Chevalier Point Pony Club and now here we are riding at Kentucky…"

"Well," Stella said, "technically you're riding at Kentucky – I'm just the girl who's holding the horse for you."

Issie looked at her best friend. "Don't say that, Stella! You know that I could never have got here without you. You've been amazing, and I don't just mean as my groom: everything you've done behind the scenes, schooling the horses and keeping them fit, making sure they are in peak condition. You've always been there for me from the very start. I don't know if I have ever told you how much it means to me…"

Stella rolled her eyes. "You haven't won yet you know, Issie! Isn't it a bit early to be giving your thank-you speech to the academy?"

Issie laughed. "Did I mention that you're also incredibly good at bringing me back to earth whenever I'm being a twit?"

"Yeah, yeah, I'm the wind beneath your wings!" Stella said as she legged Issie up on to Comet's back. "Now I put a lot of work into tacking this horse up so you just bring my boy home in one piece, OK? I'm going to be in Liberty's stall when you get back. I'll have her ready for you to ride your second clear round of the day."

Issie smiled. "Thanks again, Stella. I mean it."

"I know you do," Stella said. "Now go and kick some cross-country ass!"

"You'll report to the box at nine ten," Avery told her as they walked together towards the starting area. "I don't think you need to warm him up too much before then. Trot a bit to loosen him up and then pop him over a couple of low jumps just to get him thinking…"

"OK," Issie nodded. She was trying to listen to Avery's advice, but she was so nervous that she couldn't think straight!

She had just caught sight of one of the stars of the three-day eventing scene, Vaughn Leveritt and his magnificent chestnut, Gravitate, coming home over the final jump in the course – the Bourbon Barrels – to cross the finish line. Vaughn gave his horse a massive pat on his sleek neck as they crossed the line, but Issie could see that he looked disappointed with the ride. She understood why a few seconds later when she heard Betsy Bevan over the loudspeakers saying that Vaughn had incurred 40 faults with two refusals on the course at the Angled Rails and the Arrowheads.

He wasn't the only one to come to grief on the course already that morning. Even the more experienced riders were having run-outs and crashes. Shane Campbell had been having a brilliant round on his mare, Queen Latifah, until he reached the Squirrel Tails, where Latifah promptly took a dislike to the squirrels that earned them 20 faults.

"This course is riding much harder than everyone expected it to," Avery admitted. "The Arrowheads have caused several refusals, so remember to hold your line and aim for the flag in the distance as we discussed. And don't let him get too fast when he hits the water at the Duck Marsh – sit back and balance him, OK?"

"Uh-huh." Issie could feel the butterflies flitting about madly in her tummy now, doing loop-the-loops in formation.

Avery suddenly patted the pockets of his gilet and looked worried.

"What is it?" Issie asked.

Avery checked a second time. "I've forgotten my stopwatch," he said. He looked up at Issie. "You go ahead and take Comet over to the warm-up arena. I'll just dash back and get it and meet you there."

Avery set off at a brisk jog towards the stables and Issie walked on by herself towards the arena. She hadn't got far when she heard someone calling her name.

"Isadora!" The chubby figure of Tiggy Brocklebent, decked out in tweeds and jods, came striding vigorously across the field, with a notebook in her hands.

"I'd like a quick interview before you go out on the course," Tiggy said.

Issie hesitated. "I don't have much time, Tiggy, and I need to warm up."

"Oh, it won't take long!" Tiggy said, pulling out her pen. "Just a few quick questions."

Issie sighed. "Fine, go ahead."

"Excellent!" Tiggy said. "Now, you're riding two horses round the course today – will you be taking the same route on both of them?"

"I am," Issie said. "I plan to take a direct route straight through the big jumps on Comet and Liberty."

Tiggy looked surprised. "I expected you to take the easier options on Comet because he's so little."

"I know," Issie agreed, "but Comet can handle himself over big fences – and besides, with his little strides he's slower in the gallop than the other horses, so I can't afford to waste time by choosing the longer routes."

"You're sitting in fifth position on Blackthorn Comet and eighth on Valmont Liberty," Tiggy said. "Which horse do you rate your chances on?"

Issie froze. She didn't know what to say. She had taken Liberty on as a chance ride for the experience and to help out Marcus, but truly it was Comet that she was pinning her hopes on for glory.

Based on her cross-country track record with Liberty she would rate finishing without a broken bone as a success – but she was hardly going to tell Tiggy that!

"I can't choose between them," Issie told Tiggy. "They are both great horses. I'm very grateful to the Valmont Stables for giving me the chance ride on Liberty."

"Tactful answer," Tiggy said as if she didn't entirely believe her. She stepped closer to Comet and lowered her voice to a conspiratorial whisper. "Tell me the truth

– did you have any qualms about taking the ride on Valmont Liberty, what with the money troubles?"

"What are you talking about?" Issie said.

Tiggy's whisper grew hoarse with gossipy excitement. "I've been hearing rumours this week from some very good sources," Tiggy said. "Tyrel Valmont has what you might call a 'little problem' with failing to pay his bills. My sources say the tax department has demanded three million dollars by the end of this month, and if Valmont can't come up with the money he'll have to sell the stables!"

Tiggy saw the expression of complete shock on Issie's face.

"You didn't know about any of this?" Tiggy asked.

"No," Issie said. "Not until now."

"Valmont is determined to keep it hush-hush," Tiggy told her. "He doesn't want anyone to know that he's having financial difficulties, especially as it's not the first time. He was nearly bankrupt last year until a two-million-dollar cash injection out of the blue sorted everything out. Now he's back in trouble again… and you just happen to be his star performer."

Issie's cheeks flushed hot and she tried to pull her

thoughts together, unable to shake a feeling of growing concern. "I'm sorry, but I need to go now," she said, hurriedly looking at her watch. "I have to warm up and get ready."

"Not before you promise me the exclusive interview with you at the end of the competition!" Tiggy said. "*Horsing Around*'s readers would love to hear the story of your first Four-Star."

"Fine," Issie said. "Just let me go!"

As Issie trotted Comet back and forth in the warm-up arena she tried desperately to focus on the imposing cross-country course ahead of her, but for some reason all she could think about was Tyrel Valmont and his money problems. If what Tiggy had said was true, then Valmont was putting up a bold front when actually he was on the brink of financial ruin!

Now in possession of his stopwatch, Avery had arrived at the warm-up arena brimming with last-minute advice. "Keep your eyes constantly on your watch and check your timing markers on the course as you go," he reminded Issie. "The optimum time of sixteen minutes and ten seconds is very tight and Comet will be hard-pressed to make it. You'll need to gallop hard the whole way to—"

"Issie!" It was Marcus and Tara Kelly.

"We know you're on your way to the start box," Marcus told her. "We just came to wish you good luck."

"Thanks," Issie said. Then she asked, "If you're both here then who is back at the stables with Liberty?"

"Stella's getting her ready for your next ride," Tara said. "And I saw Mr Valmont earlier – he mentioned that he might check up on her before she competes."

"Issie!" Avery said. "We have to go. They're calling you now. You're due in the start box."

As soon as they reached the box, a white-coated steward stepped forward and grabbed Comet by the bridle, leading the skewbald into the wooden fenced-off area where he would wait until the starter set him off to begin his cross-country.

The steward looked at the little skewbald, who was already getting anxious in the small space and was clearly keen to begin. "Are you ready to go?" he asked Issie.

"No! I mean, wait! Just give me a moment!" Issie said, hanging on to Comet, who was beginning to dance about beneath her. "I just need to talk to that boy over there before I go."

She waved her hand frantically to beckon Marcus over.

"What is it?" Marcus asked as he hurried to her side.

"I need to ask you a question," Issie said. "When Valmont Promise died, was he insured?"

Marcus frowned. "Yeah. There's an insurance policy on all Valmont horses, but for Promise it was a big one, like, millions."

Issie felt her heart racing and it wasn't because she was about to ride a cross-country. "Marcus, this is important. Who got the money when Promise died?"

"Mr Valmont, of course!" Marcus said. "It was his horse!"

"And if Liberty died? Who would get the three million dollars that Liberty is insured for?"

"I…"

Marcus didn't get the chance to answer. The start-gate steward finally lost his patience. "I'm sorry, Miss Brown," he said, "but your time is up. Are you ready or do I have to disqualify you?"

Issie was starting to get a very bad feeling about Tyrel Valmont, and she had more questions to ask Marcus, but the gate steward was serious – she couldn't delay any longer.

"I'm ready," she said reluctantly, gathering up her reins and rising up in her stirrups.

"And four… three… two… one… go!" The steward's flag dropped and Issie and Comet shot forward out of the box out on to the rolling green turf of the Kentucky Four-Star cross-country course.

"Day two of the Kentucky Four-Star," Mike Partridge's voice rang out over the Tannoy. "The cross-country is underway and you're about to see the fourth competitor for the day, Isadora Brown on Blackthorn Comet, take her first fence – the Lexington Flower Box."

The Flower Box was a straightforward jump, but as Issie came towards it she pushed Comet on hard nonetheless. Avery had long ago taught her always to ride hard at the first fence. Often the horse hadn't yet woken up to the fact that he was about to start jumping and there was nothing in the world more frustrating than an unnecessary refusal at the first jump.

Issie kicked on and Comet flew the flowers, settling immediately into a powerful forward stride as they approached fence two, the Stone Walls.

The Stone Walls were a classic cross-country fence, solid and imposing. Comet popped them easily, his tail swishing as he flew the second element. He was buzzing with energy and keen to get going, his gallop opening up on the next stretch of green turf before they reached fence three, a round wooden jump known as The Mushroom.

As they bore down on the jump Issie knew that she should be focusing on riding the most important cross-country course of her entire life, but instead her mind kept leaping back to her conversation with Tiggy Brocklebent.

The journalist said Valmont was strapped for cash last year, but then miraculously received two million dollars. Was that money the insurance payout made after Valmont Promise's tragic death? And now Valmont needed three million dollars in a hurry – the exact sum he would get if Liberty died!

Was it possible that Valmont killed one of his own horses for the insurance money and was planning to do it all over again with poor Liberty? Marcus had admitted that he thought Liberty wasn't really worth three million – Valmont would never actually get that price if he tried to sell the mare. *Far better to knock her off and get the full amount.*

Issie realised a few strides out from the Mushroom that she hadn't got Comet on the right line and had to put her legs on quickly to steer him straight. The skewbald took the jump a little unbalanced and knocked it with his hind legs. The white grease on his legs helped him skim over it without injury, but Comet dropped his nose on landing and Issie had to sit back to balance him up again so he didn't fall to his knees. It was a close call and the crowd gasped as the pony very nearly came to grief.

"Oh!" Mike Partridge echoed their concern. "Almost a nasty incident there at fence number three. She's still in the saddle, but can this seventeen-year-old rider pull the Pony back together again? Because coming up we have one of the biggest spreads on this course, the Bridge."

As The Bridge loomed Issie still wasn't focused. Her brain was whirring. She was thinking back to Rio Rancho. Marcus had mentioned calling Valmont from the motel. She hadn't thought anything of it at the time, but now she realised that this meant Valmont had known exactly where they were that night. Could he have sent one of his men to dispose of Liberty there?

And what about the other night here in the stables at Kentucky Horsepark, when Marcus had fallen and broken his arm chasing the intruder? Could the hooded figure have been Valmont himself? The green passcard she'd found in the stables could easily have belonged to Valmont – his card had gone missing!

And if Valmont was now attempting to do his own dirty work then he was clearly getting more daring and more desperate as the deadline for his giant tax bill approached.

The Bridge came up suddenly in front of Issie and she kicked Comet on – one-two-three strides and hup!

"Beautifully executed over the Bridge on Blackthorn Comet," Mike Partridge trilled. "This is exactly the sort of performance we were hoping to see from this young rider hoping to make her dreams come true. Here she comes now in towards the Angled Rails and she's taken those beautifully as well! Now the long gallop round the curve of the track as she comes in to tackle the Duck Marsh…"

As Issie headed towards the water jump she didn't know what to do. She was convinced that her suspicions were right and that Valmont was responsible for Promise's death. He must have drugged Promise before the horse went out on to the cross-country course, causing the heart attack. Valmont was killing his own horses for the insurance money and he was planning to murder Liberty next!

With a sickening dread, Issie realised that Valmont was already on his way to the stables with Marcus's passcard right now. He was going to get to Liberty and dope the mare before the cross-country! Issie felt her stomach clench. Stella and Liberty were in terrible danger and Issie was the only one who knew it – and she was stuck out here, riding the most important cross-country of her entire career!

"Here she comes," Mike Partridge called out. "Isadora Brown is taking the bold, direct line straight into the

Duck Marsh just as she's done at every jump so far, and look at this pony ploughing fearlessly into the water! Three neat strides and there he goes over the wooden duck! Brilliant riding on a very narrow fence – now which way will this young rider go? Will she go left and take the long route over the low rail or right and choose the short route over the jump into the second phase of the water?"

There was a gasp of amazement from the crowd as Issie did neither. She made a sudden U-turn in the water, galloping hard back the way she had come.

"Extraordinary!" Mike Partridge said. "She's turning round completely! She must have lost her path and got confused because she's going backwards! I'm afraid the judges may be forced to penalise this. There will be time faults here and possibly elimination and… hang on a minute! What on earth… where is she going?"

The crowd of onlookers were utterly mystified by her change of direction, but Issie knew exactly what she was doing. She was no longer competing in this cross-country. She couldn't take the risk of finishing the course when there was so much at stake. The time on her stopwatch had ceased to matter – she was racing for something far more important. She had to get to the stables straight away. She had to get back – before it was too late to stop Valmont.

Chapter 12

As Issie and Comet thundered past the jump stewards and sideline officials they began shouting and waving frantically, trying to direct them back on course. On the Tannoy, Mike Partridge and Betsy Bevan were completely flummoxed.

"I've seen riders get eliminated for taking the wrong route," Betsy Bevan was telling the crowd, "but in all my years I've never seen a rider suddenly start galloping in completely the wrong direction!"

Mike Partridge spluttered. "Isadora Brown and The Pony were clear at the Duck Marsh and unbelievably they've thrown it all away! This young girl, such a great hope for the sport of eventing is now galloping for... well, we don't know where she's going!"

As she bent down over Comet's withers and urged the skewbald on, Issie ignored the shouts of the concerned onlookers and rode for all she was worth.

It had been a snap decision halfway through the water jump to turn round and go back. Had Issie really just thrown away her chance to win the Kentucky Four-Star? All that hard work, those dreams, the sacrifice and the sweat, and the future of Laurel Farm and her horses had been cast aside in one sudden, crazy moment.

What if her theories about Valmont amounted to nothing more than an over-active imagination? How would she explain herself to Stella and Avery when there had been so much riding on this for all of them? But it was too late to change her mind now. Issie's impulsiveness had already destroyed any chance she had of winning the Four-Star.

And yet in her gut, Issie was certain that she was doing the right thing. If Valmont was planning to sabotage his own horse then he would do it now, while Marcus and Tara were out of the way watching the cross-country. He would give the mare the same drug that he had given Promise and when Liberty died in the middle of the cross-country course it would look like a heart attack, just like the last time. Poor Liberty would die in front of thousands of spectators and TV cameras, and Valmont wouldn't be anywhere near her at the time. It was the ultimate alibi for a perfect crime and the only person left in Valmont's way was the young girl in Liberty's stall preparing the mare for the cross-country… Stella.

Issie stood up high in the stirrups and urged the skewbald on. They had already raced back past the Angled Rails, the Bridge and the Mushroom and now as they reached the Stone Walls, Issie veered sharply to the right and headed away from the jumps and straight towards the course barrier.

Comet took one look at the four-foot-high red and white striped barrier rails and his ears pricked forward. Finally here was something to jump at long last!

The pony flew over the barrier as if it were nothing more than a cavaletti. Issie gathered him up and pushed him up to the bridle once more, galloping on towards the stable blocks. They were now in the avenue that led to the stables and they were approaching the traffic checkpoint. In the booth ahead the security guard saw Issie and her horse coming and stepped out, raising his hand to signal its rider to stop, blowing his whistle loudly.

"Sorry!" Issie shouted at him, "this is an emergency!"

The guard's whistle let out a shocked tweet as he realised that the rider wasn't stopping. He didn't have time to raise the arm of the security gates, but it didn't matter. Comet flew over that too like any other cross-country obstacle and Issie caught a quick glimpse of the guard's stunned face as he watched her gallop past.

When they reached the end of the avenue Comet's shoes chimed out on the concrete of the stable yards and Issie knew she had no choice but to slow down – it was too risky to gallop on such an unforgiving, slippery surface. She pulled him up to a trot and they wove their way down the first row of stalls heading for Stable Block D.

When they reached the stables the wide wooden sliding doors were already open and they trotted straight inside. Liberty's loose box was down at the far end and Issie trotted Comet until they got near and then vaulted down off the skewbald's back and ran the rest of the way on foot.

"Stella!" Issie shouted as she reached Liberty's box. "Stella, are you in here? Is everything OK?"

And then Issie saw her friend. She was sprawled out in the far corner of the loose box, her red hair covering her face as she lay prone and lifeless on the straw.

"Stella!" Issie raced towards her. She wasn't moving! What had Valmont done to her?

The stomping of hooves on the straw surface of the loose box floor made Issie suddenly stop in her tracks. She turned round and saw Liberty at the other end of the stall. Tyrel Valmont was gripping her halter with one hand. In the other, he held a syringe full of lethal-looking yellow liquid. Valmont clearly hadn't been expecting to be disturbed, least of all by Issie, who was supposed to be out on the course. A horrified expression passed over his face, but then he quickly composed himself.

"Thank goodness you're here," he said unconvincingly. "I just came in and found your friend on the ground. I think the mare must have knocked her over."

He tightened his grip on Liberty's halter and took a step forward. "You look after your friend and I'll take Liberty into another stall out of your way and—"

"Let go of her!" Issie warned him. "You're not taking Liberty anywhere!"

"I'm sorry?" Valmont looked wryly amused that this young girl was standing up to him. "Are you telling me what to do with my own horse? Because I don't take orders from my staff and the last time I checked, you were working for me."

"I know what you did to Promise," Issie said, holding her ground. "I know you killed him for the insurance money."

Valmont's sense of humour disappeared. "That's a very serious claim, young lady," he said. "I'd be very careful about what accusations you make."

As he said this, Valmont let go of Liberty's halter and took a step towards Issie, and suddenly she realised that she had said too much.

"There's no need for anyone to do anything they might regret," Valmont said as he moved closer towards her, the syringe still held aloft in his hand. "Come on, let's talk about it…"

Issie took a step backwards and then another and suddenly found herself up against the wall of the stall, unable to go any further. Valmont was getting closer and closer when, out of nowhere, a dark shadow launched through the doorway of Liberty's stall.

"Mystic!"

The grey pony was suddenly right there, manouevring swiftly between Issie and Valmont, placing himself in front of the girl to protect her.

"Hoi! What do you think you're doing? Get out of here!" Valmont began waving his arms at the dapple-grey to drive him out of the loose box. But instead of shying away, Mystic went on the attack, rising up on his hind legs, front hooves flailing.

With one deft blow from his left front hoof he struck Valmont, knocking the syringe out of the man's hand and Valmont dropped to the floor clutching his wrist, howling in pain.

The grey pony stood above him, malevolent and magnificent in his anger, his nostrils flared and his ears flat back against his head.

"Get him away from me," Valmont whimpered. He was still clutching his bruised and broken wrist as he grovelled on the floor, afraid to move. "Don't let him hurt me!"

Issie ignored his pleas and went to the other end of the stall, bending down to examine Stella.

"Your friend's fine," Valmont insisted. "They were only

sleeping pills – I put them in her tea. She'll wake up soon. Now come and get this horse to leave me alone!"

It looked like Valmont was telling the truth. Stella was sound asleep and snoring. "Stella!" Issie bent over her best friend and shook her gently. "Wake up! It's me!"

"Wha… Issie?" Stella opened her eyes, "What's going on?"

"Come on, Stella!" Issie dragged her friend up to her feet. "I've got to get you out of here."

"Oh," Stella said dozily, "OK."

As she stood up she stumbled forward, still half asleep, and then reeled back again on the straw bedding. Then she looked up and saw the grey pony standing sentry over the pathetic, slumped figure of Tyrel Valmont.

"Oh, hey," Stella smiled dopily, "it's Mystic! Hi, Mystic!"

"Come on, Stella!" Issie dragged her up to her feet again. "Try to walk – I need to get you out of here."

With Stella's arm draped over her shoulder Issie managed to drag her friend out into the corridor.

Outside the stall, Issie let Stella slump down on a bench, propping her against a wall. Then, after making certain that she was OK, she went back into the loose box, grabbing a cloth from the grooming kit on the wall. She hunted around in the hay for the syringe that Valmont had dropped, carefully wrapping it in the cloth, careful not to touch it with her fingers. She was pretty sure that whatever the yellow fluid was, it had enough strength to kill a horse and would be untraceable afterwards. She was also pretty certain that the syringe would have Valmont's fingerprints all over it.

"Watch him, Mystic," she said to the grey pony as she left the stall. "I'll be right back."

Issie put the syringe in the tack room and locked it in, pocketing the key and then she headed back into the stall. Mystic was standing exactly where she had left him. Every time Valmont tried to move so much as a centimetre Mystic stamped his hooves and flicked his head back, teeth bared, as a warning that if Valmont didn't want another broken bone then he wouldn't be going anywhere.

"Good boy," Issie told the gelding. "Hold him a little longer, while I get Liberty out of here."

Since Valmont had released his hold on her the silver-dapple mare had been cooped at the back of the stall.

She stood there now tense and nervous, her flanks heaving.

"It's OK, girl," Issie tried to reassure the mare as she reached out a hand to Liberty's halter. Liberty shied back in fear as Issie reached up to take hold of her, but as Issie spoke softly to her the mare relented.

"Hey, girl," Issie murmured. "It's over now. He's not going to hurt you. You're going to be OK. It's all going to be OK."

She led Liberty out of the loose box and along the corridor, putting her in one of the empty, open stalls further down. Then she bolted off the bottom half of the Dutch door and came back to the loose box.

"Mystic..." Issie began to say as she entered the loose box, but Mystic wasn't there any more. Instead, there was a man, standing in the middle of the room with Tyrel Valmont and he didn't look pleased to see her.

"You're the girl that jumped the barrier!" It was the security guard who Issie had ignored when she jumped the security gate. He must have followed her and Comet all the way down the driveway and hunted through the stables to find them.

"I can explain everything," Issie said to him.

"It better be a good story," the guard said. He was pink-faced and puffed from running after her.

"I had to get back to help my groom." Issie pointed out into the corridor where Stella could now be seen lying back against the stable wall, snoring with her mouth wide open.

"That man next to you knocked her out with sleeping pills and then tried to kill his own horse."

The security guard's eyes grew wide. This girl had nearly mown him down on her horse just a moment ago. Now he'd arrived here to find her with some red-headed kid on a bench in the corridor snoring and drooling on her T-shirt, and one of the wealthiest and most powerful men in the eventing business lying in the straw with a broken wrist. What was going on?

"Please, you have to believe me!" Issie said. "Tyrel Valmont is a horse murderer!"

"This is preposterous," Tyrel Valmont interrupted as he stood up, wincing in pain at his broken wrist. He looked at the guard. "I'm the head of the Valmont Stables. I could have your job for this. Now get out of my way and let me go—"

"Wait!" Issie said. "I can show you proof. I've got the syringe of poison that he used to try and kill Liberty. It's locked up in the tack room!"

Valmont went to push past the security guard, but the guard put up a hand and blocked his path.

"I'm sorry, Mr Valmont," the guard said, "but this young lady here seems pretty upset. You just hang tight in here for a moment, sir, while I check out her story."

Issie went to the tack room and brought out the syringe, which she handed to the security guard.

The guard looked at the vial filled with yellow fluid and then set it aside for a moment and dialled his phone. "Hello, police? It's Kyle Jones here. Yeah, I'm on security detail at the Kentucky Horsepark. Can I get a squad car sent straight away? There's been an accusation of attempted murder… Yes, ma'am – Mr Tyrel Valmont… No, ma'am, not a person; apparently he tried to kill a horse. Yes, ma'am, that's right – a horse. You heard me – A HORSE. For Pete's sake – just send the squad car, OK!"

The guard hung up the phone and turned to Issie. "You better not be pulling my leg – they think I'm crazy down at the station!"

"Thank you," Issie said gratefully. "It's the truth. You'll see."

The police arrived fifteen minutes later – at the same time as Avery, Marcus and Tara reached the stables.

Valmont tried to smooth-talk his way out of it, insisting he was innocent. But the hard evidence of the syringe, combined with the businessman's debts and the unsolved death of Valmont Promise, was all they needed to charge Tyrel Valmont and take him into custody.

"So where is Liberty? Are you sure she's OK?" Marcus asked.

Issie nodded. "She'll be totally fine. Valmont didn't have a chance to inject her. I put her in an empty stall."

Marcus hurried off to check on the mare. Avery, meanwhile, was bent over Stella, who was finally beginning to wake up from the sleeping pills that Valmont had put in her drink.

"Tom! What are you doing here?" Stella slurred in a sleepy voice. "Do you want me to groom Mystic too?"

Avery frowned. "What are you talking about, Stella?"

He knelt down beside her. "It's OK, try to relax. You've been drugged. We'll take you to hospital and get you checked out."

"OK," Stella said. "Hospital good. But first I'm just going to have a little, little catnap…" She slumped back down on the bench again.

"Tom," Issie said. "I'm really sorry about riding off like that in the middle of the course. I know I ruined everything…"

Avery looked at her, completely stunned. "I must admit it gave me a shock at the time, but, Issie, I totally understand why you did it now! You can't possibly think that I'd be angry at you for wanting to save Stella's life?"

Issie shook her head. "But Tom, the prize money! This was our chance to—"

She was interrupted by the sound of hooves in the corridor as Marcus and Tara led Liberty out to join them.

"I've checked her over and she seems to be fine," Marcus said.

"Good," Tara said to him. "I'll call the vet in to do a blood test just to be safe, but in the meantime you'd better get to work."

"You want me to do it?" Marcus asked.

"Well, Stella can't possibly manage in her condition. Can she?" Tara pointed out. She looked at her watch. "You've got plenty of time. She's not scheduled to go until one twenty."

Marcus nodded. "OK, I'll start bandaging her legs."

Issie turned to Tara. "What's going on? What is Marcus doing?"

"He's taking over as your groom," Tara replied. "We're getting your horse ready."

"You're joking."

"I'm deadly serious," Tara said. "Liberty is still in the game, Issie, and so are you. In two hours you're going to be back out there – riding the cross-country."

Chapter 13

Issie had turned her back on eventing glory, giving up her dream to save Stella and Liberty. After abandoning the cross-country mid-competition she never thought that she'd be given a second chance.

Tara, however, saw matters differently. "Liberty is still entered in this competition," she pointed out. "You're still registered to ride her."

"But what about Valmont?" Issie asked.

"The police are charging Tyrel Valmont with financial fraud and attempted horse murder," Tara said. "However, you and Liberty aren't being charged with anything. Officially, you still have every right to go ahead and ride her. It's up to you, Issie – what do you want to do?"

"Even if I wanted to do it, the judges will never let me ride again!" Issie said. "After the way I tore off on Comet there's no way I'd be allowed back on the course. I've probably been banned from ever riding in a Four-Star again."

"Leave it with me," Avery said. "Once I explain the situation to Blaire Andrews I'm certain they'll be more than sympathetic to your plight."

Avery looked at Issie. "You can pull out if you really want to, Issie. I would understand completely, and so would Tara and Marcus, after the ordeal you've just been through. But the opportunity is here if you want to take it. It's up to you."

Issie looked at him and grinned. "Are you kidding, Tom? Of course I want to!"

With that decision made, everyone was swiftly allocated their roles. There was much to be done over the next two hours before the mare was due in the start box. Avery headed off to clear the paperwork with Blaire Andrews, Marcus took on the preparation of Liberty and Tara went to check on Stella, who was being cared for by the St John's medics, who were on site, monitoring the cross-country. It was left up to Issie to take care of Comet.

After his mad gallop the skewbald needed a good wash-down to get the sweat off him. Issie took her pony to the wash bay and hosed him all over, then used the sweat-scraper to squeegee off excess moisture before walking Comet to keep his muscles from getting too chilly as he dried off. She rugged him up afterwards in his woollen stable blanket and then took him back to his loose box where hard feed was already in the feed bin waiting for him.

Comet, true to form, stuck his muzzle straight into the feed bin and began to hoover down his supper greedily.

"You've certainly earnt it this time," Issie told him as she watched him devouring the barley and sugar beet. She gave Comet a pat on his damp chestnut and white neck.

Through all the drama that morning, it was only just dawning on Issie that she had thrown away her chance on the talented skewbald.

"We never did get to show them, did we, Comet?" she murmured to the pony. "I'm so sorry, boy, I know you deserved to win. If I hadn't dragged you off like I did then you would have gone clear."

Comet lifted his head out of the feed bin for a moment and looked at Issie with his big, soft brown eyes. Then he gave a snort as if to say, "Don't worry about it – I'm over it already!"

Issie giggled. "You're right, Comet. There'll be other cross-countries. You and I will get another chance."

Right now, though, Issie still had a chance of her own on her second ride. Somehow, she had to put the incredible events of the morning behind her and pull herself together. Liberty was waiting for her.

Issie had been worried that Liberty would be more shaken by her ordeal, but the mare had trusted Valmont and didn't seem to realise the extreme danger she had been in. When Issie arrived at Liberty's loose box she found Marcus trying to tack the mare up, but he was having problems with his arm encased in plaster. He was fumbling with the tendon boots and couldn't do up the buckles.

"Here," Issie said gently, "I'll do it."

"It's just so frustrating!" Marcus complained.

"They're only tendon boots, it's no big deal," Issie said.

"Not the boots," Marcus sighed, "I mean this!"

He held his plaster cast up in the air with a look of despair on his face. Issie suddenly realised just how awful this must be for him, having to sit on the sidelines and watch while she rode the horse that should have been his.

"I'm sorry," she said softly. "It should be you out there today – not me."

Marcus took a deep breath and pulled himself together. "No," he said. "This mare owes you her life. You deserve to ride her today."

"Marcus." Issie looked worried. "I don't know if I can do it. I've only had one practice ride on her and you saw how badly it went."

"You'll be OK," Marcus reassured her. "Liberty is the best cross-country horse I've ever ridden. She's bold and strong. She's so powerful she almost pulled my arms out of their sockets the last time I rode her round a course."

He looked at Issie. "Issie, you can win with this mare. But you'll need to change the way you ride if you're going to make it clear and inside the time. Listen very carefully – because I'm going to tell you what to do…"

In the start box the silver-dapple mare moved anxiously, crab-stepping from side to side. Issie took a tighter grip on the reins as she watched the steward speak into his walkie-talkie to check that the course ahead was clear.

"OK," he told Issie, "we have confirmation. You're good to go. Are you ready?"

Issie could feel her heart pounding like it was trying to escape from her chest. She looked over at Marcus, who was standing on the sidelines. He gave Issie the thumbs-up signal and she waved back. After their talk during the tacking up, she had agreed to go with his game plan for the cross-country. It was risky and Issie knew it, but then Marcus knew the mare better than anyone – if this was the way he wanted Issie to ride Liberty, then she had to trust him. More than that, she had to trust the horse beneath her.

"Are you ready, Liberty?" Issie whispered to the mare. She could feel Liberty's body quivering in anticipation. She took a deep breath and looked out from the start box at the smooth green turf that led to the first fence.

"I'm ready," she told the steward. Issie took an even tighter hold on Liberty's reins with one hand, the other holding at her own wrist in preparation to press the stopwatch. She stood up in her stirrups in two-point position like a jockey, as the steward counted her down.

"And four… three… two… one… go!"

Liberty broke from the box like a Thoroughbred. As the mare surged forward Issie felt a rush of adrenalin and, for the second time that day, she suddenly found herself facing down the Kentucky Four-Star cross-country.

As they approached the first fence, Issie thought

back to that conversation she'd had with Marcus. Now she was on the course she understood with shocking clarity what Marcus had been trying to tell her. She could feel the pure, brute strength of the mare beneath her as Liberty began tanking, leaning so heavily on Issie's hands that it felt like her arms were going to be wrenched off.

Marcus was right, Issie would never be strong enough to hold back a horse like Liberty for six whole kilometres of cross-country jumps. "It would be fatal to try to hold her back," Marcus had told her in the stables. "She's more powerful than you are, Issie – if you try to control her you'll never win."

"So what should I do then?" Issie said.

"Let her go," Marcus replied. "Don't try to hold her back or fight her. Just go with her."

"Are you kidding?" Issie's eyes grew wild. "Liberty could bolt on me! I'll be on a cross-country course with a horse that is barely in control."

"If you try and slow Liberty down then you'll lose the Four-Star," Marcus said. "There's no way you can make it in the optimum time if you fight her back or take the long routes. But if you go straight and let her go – if you trust her to handle the jumps at a gallop, stay with her and kick on – then you just might make it."

As she jumped the Flower Box for the second time that day, Issie marvelled at the differences between cheeky Comet and silver-dappled Liberty. The mare wasn't a natural jumper like Comet, but she was incredibly well schooled. It was clear that Marcus had spent hours and hours drilling her so that technically you couldn't fault her style. While Comet tended to bound all over the place like an eager puppy, Liberty wasted absolutely no excess energy over a jump, always judging it precisely and never giving more than a centimetre of clearance above the rails. The grease on her legs came into effect by the time they had reached the Mushroom. Issie heard the scrape of the mare's hind legs as she slid over it. Liberty was a pro and she knew exactly how to handle every obstacle. It was the same at the Bridge. Issie aimed the mare dead centre on the sweet spot and Liberty didn't waste any time before she was back in a gallop again and racing towards the next fence.

It was just like Avery had said – now that Liberty's blood was up and she was on the course for real, she was a totally different horse. Perhaps Liberty also understood somehow that Issie had saved her life that morning. Whatever it was, there was a bond of trust between Issie and Liberty that hadn't been there before and the mare felt confident and bold as they approached the Duck Marsh.

It took all of Issie's strength to slow Liberty down enough to balance her up to jump the wooden duck in the water and then turn her hard left to leap out over the wooden rails before circling back through the water and up the bank towards the next jump, the Hickory Tables.

"Beautifully executed by Isadora Brown riding Valmont Liberty!" Mike Partridge told the crowd. "Those of you who have been here all day at the Duck Marsh will remember that this is the same rider who turned her last horse, Blackthorn Comet, round *in the middle of the pond* and abandoned the course and galloped for home. But not this time! It looks like the runaway rider has broken her jinx. She's successfully through the Duck Marsh on her second mount of the day, Valmont Liberty, and my word, what a ride this mare is giving the young lady! Look at them go!"

Mike Partridge didn't know the half of it. Liberty emerged from the water jump at a full gallop. The mare had decided that she was no longer interested in slowing down for the fences. She was bolting and even if Issie wanted to, she couldn't have stopped her.

Steeling herself, Issie remembered Marcus's game plan. *Don't fight the mare when it happens, just hang in there and go with her.* It was a theory that worked OK for big, simple jumps like the Hickory Tables, but as Issie got further round the course she began to experience some very hairy moments! At the Giant Squirrel Tails, Issie found herself executing a high-speed turn between the tails and hanging on for dear life as Liberty only realised that she needed to take a second jump when the next squirrel loomed suddenly into view. They made it over, though, and at the second water complex Liberty ploughed into the Lake so fast she sent up a wake that almost drenched the spectators on the sideline. As they headed up the hill towards the Sheep Shelter they were still clear and going strong.

Still to come, though, was the biggest fence on the course, the Gamekeeper's Brush. So far, Liberty had managed to get away with galloping hard at the jumps without being checked and had taken off on a solid forward stride every time. But the Gamekeeper's Brush was no ordinary fence. Issie knew the spread was two metres seventy wide! One mistake, one-last minute flub or a hoof out of line at the speed that Liberty was now travelling, would be nothing short of catastrophic. If Issie thought the cracked ribs she was nursing right now were bad, that was nothing compared to what would happen at the Gamekeeper's Brush if they got it wrong.

This was the most dangerous thing Issie had ever done in her life. As they galloped down the hill towards the Gamekeeper's Brush Issie knew without a shadow of a doubt that this fence could kill her. If Liberty got her timing wrong and tried to chip in an extra stride at the last minute then she wouldn't have time to lift her legs for take-off and would slam into the rails that supported the hedge, cartwheel backwards and land on top of Issie in the ditch.

Issie felt the knot in her stomach tighten in a way she had never experienced before. Something was very wrong and as the fence grew closer she suddenly realised what it was. As the ditch loomed ahead of them, she felt a chill run down her spine. Liberty was coming at the jump in a mad gallop – and she was on the wrong stride.

Chapter 14

Issie had no more than a split-second to solve the situation. If she kept going on the wrong stride Liberty would find herself too close to the fence on take-off and she would crash. If Issie pulled the mare off the jump, veering to the side of the ditch, it would be counted as a refusal and would put them out of the competition. But at least they'd still be alive.

But Issie had come too far to throw it away now. There had to be another way.

Steeling herself, Issie suddenly put her legs on and rode even harder at the jump. Ignoring the ditch, she raised her eyes to look at the brush, growling encouragement to the horse beneath her, asking the mare to go even faster and increase her stride!

It was an incredibly risky decision and the crowd on the sidelines knew it. You could hear them collectively holding their breath while Mike Partridge's voice came tense and shrill over the loudspeaker. "Oh… my goodness… she's coming in very, very fast indeed. This mare had better not put a foot wrong!"

Issie's urgings did exactly what she hoped they would do. Liberty had stretched out, altering her stride so that by the time she reached the jump, she found herself at the perfect take-off mark. The mare never even noticed the ditch below her as she pricked her ears and leapt, arcing beautifully over the enormous spread as if it wasn't even there to clear the jump with ease.

Taking the massive spread was almost like flying. And then they were back on the ground again on the other side and galloping on, Issie with her heart hammering at a million times the normal rate. She had done it! It was the biggest fence she'd ever taken in her life and they'd jumped it! She felt a brief moment of utter elation at having made it over – and then realised just how crucial it was to gather her wits once more. The very worst thing a cross-country rider could do was get cocky, even for a moment, while still on the course. There were six fences to come before she made it home and she couldn't afford to underestimate any of them. Especially since the silver-dapple mare was beginning to tire now, after galloping flat out for five kilometres. This was the danger zone, the final quarter of the course, when the horses began to flag and accidents were most likely to happen.

Issie knew that Liberty must have been exhausted, and yet the mare was so strong! Issie still had no brakes. As they came up to the next jump, the Tobacco Stripping Table, she shortened up the reins a little to alert Liberty that there was a serious obstacle ahead. The flat-topped wooden table was supposed to be taken as a big spread, but Liberty had other ideas. She sprang up on to the table like a cat jumping up on to the kitchen bench and then leapt back off again down the other side to the wild applause of the crowd, who thought it was brilliantly funny!

"Well done!" Issie gave Liberty a slappy pat on her sweaty neck as they galloped on. It didn't matter that they had taken the jump in an unconventional fashion – as long as they were over it, that was fine!

At the Normandy Bank, Liberty popped through the complex in much more classic style and once again the crowd cheered, as did Mike Partridge.

"Now this is the way the Normandy Bank should be ridden!" the announcer trilled over the loudspeakers. "In fact this is shaping up to be a very stylish round here at Kentucky by this gifted seventeen-year-old rider. Now, with just four fences to come, can Isadora Brown bring this mare home?"

As Mike Partridge asked the question, Issie and Liberty flew over the Tudor Cottages and the crowd shouted them on. There were only two fences to come and as she galloped along the final sward of green turf towards the finish line Liberty felt as powerful as ever. They were coming up to a course marker and Issie took a moment to check her stopwatch. She had been expecting to be ahead of the clock because of Liberty's strong galloping and she was shocked to see that in fact they were almost exactly on the time. If they lost even a second over the next two fences then they would fall behind and incur faults. She had to press on!

The Kentucky Hedge was a clean and simple jump, but Issie was careful not to underestimate it. A refusal at the second to last obstacle in the competition would have been totally heartbreaking.

"She's clear over the Kentucky Hedge and here she comes!" Betsy Bevan called out. "Look at this young jockey showing riders twice her age how it should be done! She's coming up to the last jump and – look at the clock as she approaches the Bourbon Barrels! It will be touch and go right down to the finish line!"

As Liberty took the barrels Issie was already up and over the mare's withers, urging her on as hard as she could for the final gallop to the line. They flew past the flags and as they did so Issie closed her fingers round her stopwatch, clicking the timer off. For a moment, as Liberty slowed to a trot, Issie couldn't bring herself to look at the watch display. And then, when she finally drew her eyes to it, a smile spread across her face. They were home. They were clear. And they had made it a whole second inside the required time!

As Avery, Marcus and Tara rushed towards her, Issie vaulted off her horse and let her team take over the important job of cooling down her mount.

"Brilliant round!" was all Avery said as he took the reins from her and began to lead Liberty at a walk, keeping the mare moving so that she wouldn't stiffen up.

Issie collapsed on the grass, chest heaving and ribs aching, while her pit crew did their jobs. Tara was busily stripping off Liberty's tack and throwing a cooler rug over the mare's quarters to stop her getting a chill, while Marcus was working on the front end and where the saddle had been, vigorously sponging the mare down.

"She's got a small cut on her stifle. She must have scraped her hindquarters over a couple of the fences," Marcus said to Tara. "We'll have to keep an eye on her for signs of swelling."

"I'll check her thoroughly when I get her back to the loose box," Tara confirmed. "Tom needs another five to cool her before I can take over."

"Issie!"

It was Stella. She looked puffy-faced and exhausted but smiling nonetheless as she ran over to join Issie with Shane Campbell by her side.

"That was an amazing round," Stella said. "Sorry I wasn't there to help you get her ready."

"I'm just glad you're OK," Issie said. "You are OK, aren't you?"

"The paramedic guys say I'm fine," Stella said. "I can't even really remember anything. One minute I'm having a cup of tea and then the next thing I know I'm in an ambulance. But my head feels totally clear now."

"She should still be lying down, if you ask me," Shane said protectively, "but she won't listen. She insisted on being here to help with Liberty."

Stella ignored this comment. "I was watching you on the round on the closed-circuit TV in the ambulance," she told Issie. "That was a killer round! You were totally galloping flat out the whole way."

"Yeah," Issie said. "That wasn't exactly my idea. I

could barely control Liberty most of the time – all I did was hang on!"

"Well, whatever you did, it worked," Stella said. "So far only six riders have made it within time and—"

Stella broke off mid-sentence. As they'd been talking she'd been watching Avery still diligently leading Liberty around. "What is he doing?" she muttered, "He's taking too long. They should be getting the ice boots on her now!"

Stella turned to Shane. "Can you go and get Liberty's ice boots ready? They're in her loose box. I'll come and help you in a minute."

Shane hurried off to sort out the ice boots and Stella turned back to Issie. "I was kind of spaced out by the sleeping pills," she said. "But Tom explained what happened in the stables – I know what you did for me, giving up your chance of winning on Comet to save me. I don't know how to thank you."

"Hey, Stell? You're not going to get mushy on me, are you?" Issie smiled. "Now, go and take care of Liberty. I'm relying on you."

At this moment in the competition, Stella was the most vital person on Issie's team. Liberty had just been through a punishing cross-country and she would need expert care to recover in time for the showjumping tomorrow. The next twenty-four hours were crucial and Stella was in charge. Back at the loose box she got the team to work, fitting ice boots on all four legs to soothe the pain and control the swelling. Over the next four hours Stella and Marcus would be constantly refilling and replacing the boots on Liberty's legs. Tara would also be massaging the mare vigorously all over to ease her aches and pains.

It was nearly one in the morning when Issie turned up at the stables to see how the mare was doing and Stella was still there, bandaging Liberty's legs and giving her another serving of hard feed.

"Stella, you shouldn't be working like this after everything you've been through," Issie said. "Go back to our cabin and get some rest."

"No, thanks. I've had more than enough sleep to last me a while," Stella said. She bent down again over Liberty's legs and massaged them just above the bandages. "I tried trotting her on the concrete just now to see if she was sound and she looked a bit stiff in the hindquarters."

The second trotting-up was always held on the morning of the showjumping day, to test whether the horses were sound enough to continue after the gruelling trials of the cross-country. Any sign of lameness and a horse would be 'spun' – which meant disqualification on the spot.

"I'm sure Liberty will come right by the morning," Issie reassured Stella. "Horses are always stiff after the cross-country. Anyway, there's nothing more you can do for her now."

"OK," Stella said reluctantly, picking up her bandages and brushes and heading for the stable door. "I'll be back here at six a.m., though, to check on her legs and start plaiting her up."

She looked at Issie, who was still standing with the mare, stroking her silvery-blonde mane. "Are you coming? You must be exhausted too."

"I'll catch you up," Issie said. "I won't be long."

She wanted to spend a moment alone in the stall with Liberty. The mare had tried so hard for her out there on the cross-country course. She had rewarded Issie's trust in her by never faltering or stopping, and although at times it had been terrifying, the mare had delivered one of the most exhilarating cross-country rounds that Issie had ever ridden. It was hard to believe that if Issie hadn't turned back on Comet to come to Liberty's aid, then this mare wouldn't be here right now.

Of course, Issie realised only too well that if it hadn't been for Mystic, then she might not be here now either. Mystic had saved her from Valmont. Once again the grey pony had been there just when she needed him most. Afterwards, Avery had told Issie that Valmont raved and complained to the police about being attacked by a dapple-grey who flew at him out of the blue and broke his wrist.

"He must have meant that Liberty struck him," Avery said. "She's a silver-dapple so perhaps the police got it confused."

"Maybe," Issie replied.

Tyrel Valmont was in a prison cell awaiting his arraignment. Meanwhile, the board of directors at the Valmont Stables had already ousted him, and Tara Kelly had told Issie that even if the charges didn't stick, there was no way that Valmont would ever return to run the stables.

"He can't hurt you any more, girl," Issie reassured Liberty as she put her rug on and switched out the light.

As she walked back through the stable blocks in the dark, Issie could have sworn she caught sight of a horse in the darkness. For a brief moment she saw him there watching her, the familiar coal-black eyes in a snow-white face with their gaze trained upon her. She smiled to herself and kept walking, safe in the knowledge that he was there with her.

Chapter 15

It was still dark at 6 a.m. when the phone rang. Bleary-eyed and half asleep, Issie fumbled about on her bedside table and finally found her mobile. When she answered it she was stunned to hear mad screaming at the other end of the line.

"Ohmygod! Ohmygod! Ohmygod!" It was Kate.

"I just turned on the radio and heard the news! You're in second place? And you're riding some horse I've never even heard of? Why didn't you call to tell us all of this?"

It was true. Issie was in second place on Liberty! The cross-country course had proved to be one of the most challenging in the long history of the Kentucky Four-Star and by the end of the day, once the cross-country scores had been added to the tally, many of the frontrunners after the dressage had found themselves either eliminated or with refusal faults that made them slide down the rankings.

With a clear round and no time faults Issie and Liberty had moved up the rankings from eighth to an incredible second place! They were going into the showjumping ring today just two points behind the leader, Gerhardt Muller, the Austrian rider whose stallion, Avatar, had put in a neat cross-country round to maintain their lead.

"So who is this horse you're riding? And what happened when you were riding Comet?" Kate asked. "Why did you turn round in the middle of the course?"

Issie gave Kate a very brief version of the Valmont story – about the attempted murder of Liberty, and why she abandoned the cross-country on Comet.

"Ohmygod!" Kate said. "Is Stella OK?"

"She's fine," Issie said glancing over at Stella, who was still asleep. "She's been up half the night looking after Liberty. We've got the trot-up in a couple of hours. Stella was worried because Liberty was a bit stiff last night."

"You'll get through it," Kate said. "I know you will. It would just be too cruel if you got spun now!"

"Even if we do get through," Issie said, "don't get excited. There are loads of riders right behind me on the points table… all I need to do is drop a rail and it's all over."

"Of course I'm excited!" Kate squealed. "They're screening the showjumping live on TV in New Zealand, Dan and Ben and I are getting together to watch it. And all the little kids at pony club are so excited that someone from Chevalier Point is riding at the Kentucky Four-Star – they can't believe I actually know you!"

By the time she hung up the phone Issie had promised Kate that she would be a guest instructor at a Chevalier Point Pony Club rally the next time she was home in New Zealand. She was just about to jump in the shower when the mobile rang again. This time it was her mother. Mrs Brown was completely and utterly beside herself with excitement. "I was just sitting here watching the news," Mrs Brown squeaked, "and you were on TV! They said you're in second place at Kentucky!"

Issie was amazed. "I was on the news?"

"There was footage of you jumping some enormous ditch!" Mrs Brown said. "It looked terrifying to me!"

Issie had to smile. Her mum knew nothing about horses and even a cavaletti looked terrifying to her, but for once she had to agree.

"It was a pretty scary fence, but we made it. We went clear."

"Even Aidan thought it looked like a big jump," her mother added. "He called me just after the news was on. He said to tell you good luck. He also said that half of Gisborne is going round to Hester's house to watch you in the showjumping—"

"Issie!" Stella interrupted the call. "Come on! Get in the shower already! We've got the trotting-up in half an hour!"

"Mum," Issie said, "I've got to go now. But I'll call you soon."

There was silence on the other end of the phone for a moment and then Issie heard her mother's voice, all choked up. "I'm so proud of you, sweetie."

"Thanks, Mum," Issie said.

"Good luck!" Mrs Brown said. "We'll all be watching you."

Issie hung up. *We'll all be watching you.* She would already be facing a stadium full of twenty-thousand spectators and TV cameras and now she would be carrying the expectations of her friends and family and every pony-club kid in New Zealand with her.

And Issie had even greater pressures on her. She didn't want to tell her mum just how tight the financial situation had become at Laurel Farm, but the truth was, if she didn't win today then her future on the international eventing circuit would be uncertain at best. She might be home in Chevalier Point and giving guest lessons at the pony club sooner than anyone realised.

The crowds had gathered at the trotting-up grounds by the time Issie and Liberty arrived. Issie stood in front of the judges with the mare at her side and looked at the strip of tarmac ahead of her. When the order to trot came, she took a deep breath and put herself in the hands of fate. Whatever happened now, it was for the best. If Liberty was sore then it was far better to find out now and be spun than to carry on and jump the mare and risk hurting her.

"Isadora Brown. Whenever you're ready, you may trot," a white-coated steward gave Issie the nod and she began running, with Liberty trotting right beside her. She didn't dare to look at the mare – it was important that she keep her eyes straight ahead and try and keep the mare moving rhythmically. She could hear Liberty's hooves striking the tarmac in a solid trit-trot beat and she hoped that the judges weren't spotting any problems.

She reached the end of the tarmac strip and turned the mare and then trotted back again. The three judges stood and watched the display in silence, making notes on their pads and then conferring with one another. Then the head judge raised a thumb in the air and the confirmation came over the loudspeaker to the crowd who had gathered to watch.

"Isadora Brown and Valmont Liberty have been passed for the next phase!"

The relief and the excitement of getting through was even greater than Issie had realised. Suddenly the tight knot of nerves that had been building in her tummy all morning disappeared.

The showjumping began in just a couple of hours but, since they were sitting in second place and these events ran in reverse order of ranking, that meant she would be the second-to-last competitor to ride.

Or at least that was what she thought, until Stella raced over with some dramatic news.

"Avatar has been spun!"

"What?" Issie couldn't believe it. "You're kidding me!"

Stella shook her head. "It's official. Gerhardt Muller says the stallion had a really bad knock on the Tobacco Stripping Table and now he's favouring his off-hind. The judges had no choice. They put him in the holding box to reconsider and Gerhardt's withdrawn him."

Issie was stunned. With Avatar and Gerhardt Muller out of the competition she was now by default in first place! The knot in her tummy was returning big-time! A clear round had suddenly become more important than ever – Issie was riding with $100,000 right there within her grasp. Victory was now so close – and she had everything to lose.

Earlier, Marcus had walked the course with Issie on foot and they had discussed the best way to approach the jumps. Now, while Stella tacked Liberty up, he stood by with last-minute advice.

"I don't know if you want to hear this," Marcus said, "but so far this season showjumping hasn't been Liberty's best phase. She has a tendency to disregard the poles and drop her hind legs. When we were competing at the Fair Hill Three-Star she took down eight rails."

"Eight rails!" Issie's heart sank. "That's not a showjumping round – that's a demolition derby!"

A single rail down was all it would take to put her out of the running and Marcus was telling her that this mare treated the showjumping course as if the jumps were skittles and she was the bowling ball!

"The last event was two months ago and I've schooled her loads and loads since then to try and improve her," Marcus pointed out. "And you rode Liberty to a clear round yesterday when other horses were being eliminated left and right. You can do this too."

"You seem to have a lot of faith in me," Issie frowned, "and I've got no idea why."

"That's because you don't realise how special you are," Marcus smiled at her. "But I do."

The crowd in the stadium at the Kentucky Four-Star let out a cheer as the final rider of the day entered the arena to begin her round.

"And here she is at last," the voice of Mike Partridge crackled to life over the loudspeaker, "Isadora Brown and her chance ride Valmont Liberty. What a competition it has been for this combination! As this seventeen-year-old girl enters the arena on this magnificent mare, they are the very picture of a balanced partnership. It is hard to believe that Isadora only sat on this horse for the very first time four days ago and now here they are…"

As they rode into the stadium, Issie heard the roar of the crowd and felt the mare surge forward beneath her. Liberty was keen to jump, and despite what Marcus had just told her, Issie had faith in the mare. Her trust in Liberty's abilities had got them this far. Now, more than just trust in her horse, she also needed to have faith in herself. She needed to put aside the pressure and focus on the task at hand.

As the bell rang, Issie tipped her hat to the judges and pushed Liberty on into a canter through the flags. As soon as the mare soared the first fence without so much as dusting it with her hooves Issie felt her tension disappear. The weight of the world lifted off her shoulders and she found herself remembering something that she had almost lost sight of in the past few days – that she loved this sport more than anything in the world. She felt the joy of it now as Liberty took the fence cleanly and then put in the most exquisite flying change to canter on the opposite leg and turn to ride at the treble. One-and-two-and-three! Issie cleared the three jumps without touching a rail. They took two more fences cleanly and then there was a gasp from the crowd as Liberty dropped a fetlock and scraped a rail on jump number nine. The pole rocked in the metal socket, but it didn't fall and a universal sigh of relief rippled through the stadium.

And then there were just three jumps left. Issie kept her hands steady and her legs on as she took one jump and then the next and then she was coming up to the big blue-railed oxer that marked the end of the course.

"This is it!" stage-whispered the announcer. The tension was unbearable and Mike Partridge was utterly beside himself. "One final jump to go and this young girl becomes the youngest rider ever to win one of the world's great equestrian events. Can she do it?"

Issie looked at the fence ahead of her and saw Liberty's ears swivel forward in eagerness. She held her position in the saddle, counted the strides and let the mare go at exactly the right moment. Liberty took her cue and arced up in the perfect bascule, rounding herself over the jump in textbook fashion. They were clear! The silver-dapple mare raced through the flags to the wild applause of the crowd and the jubilant voice of the announcer on the loudspeakers. "Isadora Brown and Valmont Liberty have just won the Kentucky Four-Star!"

Chapter 16

As the crowd erupted in the stands Issie rode Liberty round the arena standing up in her stirrups and taking off her helmet to wave it above her head in salute.

"What a performance!" Mike Partridge was in full revelry. "Four days ago Isadora Brown sat on this mare for the very first time and now her chance ride has taken her all the way to the top. Look at the expression of total disbelief on this young rider's face as it dawns on her that she has just claimed one of the greatest prizes in the eventing world!"

Mike Partridge was still raving as Issie finished the lap and rode back out into the wings where Avery, Stella, Tara and Marcus were waiting for her.

Avery was so excited that he actually punched his fist in the air. "Fantastic stuff! That was a textbook clear round!" Avery said. "The best you've ever ridden."

"Faultless and fabulous!" Tara agreed.

It was Marcus who shocked her the most, though. As Issie vaulted down from Liberty's back he came running up to her. "I can't believe how brilliant you are!" Marcus grinned. And then, out of the blue, he planted a kiss on her lips. It was only a quick peck, spurred on by the excitement of the moment, but Issie felt a jolt of electricity go through her as their lips touched.

"Ohmygod!" Stella was suddenly beside Issie, her eyes wild with excitement. "Issie! You've just won a hundred thousand dollars! We're rich! That's enough to pay all our bills and—"

"Wait a minute," Tara interrupted Stella's feverish rant. "It's more complicated than that, I'm afraid. Liberty has just won a hundred thousand dollars, but Issie was riding on behalf of the Valmont Stables – and as the rider she's only due ten per cent of the prize money. The rest will go to the mare's owners."

Stella's face dropped. "You can't be serious!"

"I'm sorry." Tara looked almost as upset as Stella did.

"It's not my decision – this is how the business works. Tom and I arranged the paperwork with Valmont Stables when Issie signed the contract to ride the mare."

Issie didn't know what to say. She remembered signing the documents that Avery had brought her when he organised everything with Blaire Andrews and there was a clause about the prize money. But she hadn't thought about it really at the time because she never thought she would win on Liberty. Of course it made sense for the horse's owners to get the lion's share of the prize. Her ten per cent was still ten thousand dollars, but it was nowhere near enough money to cover their costs. Certainly not enough to prevent her from having to sell Nightstorm.

Suddenly the moment of glory wasn't quite so glowing. Issie had done everything that she possibly could and had actually won the Kentucky Four-Star. It was strange, to be swept up in this moment of pure elation and joy and at the same time to know that it still wasn't enough to save them.

"Issie! Issie Brown!"

There was a shout from the crowds as a short, squat blonde woman pushed her way through the barriers, vigorously flashing her press pass to the security guards so that they would let her through. It was Tiggy Brocklebent.

"Congratulations, Issie!" Tiggy said as she tottered across the grass towards her. "Now tell me that you haven't spoken to anyone else yet! Remember, you promised me an exclusive for *Horsing Around* magazine!"

"Tiggy?" Issie was stunned. "I've only just ridden out of the arena. Of course I haven't spoken to anyone else yet!"

"Well you can't be too careful!" Tiggy said. "Paparazzi! They'll be after you like vultures now, you know. All the magazines and newspapers will want a piece of you. Not to mention the sponsors."

"Sponsors?"

"Yes, my dear," Tiggy said, "the ones with the big cheque books! A win at Kentucky puts you in the A-list. They'll be queuing up to offer you deals. All the clothing brands will want you wearing their jodhpurs and the feed companies will shower you with products and beg you to endorse their lucerne chaff." Tiggy looked Issie in the eyes. "Whatever you do, don't you let them rope you into a contract for anything less than half a million. That's what a star rider like you is worth on the open market!"

"Erm, you're joking!"

"I'm most certainly not!" Tiggy insisted. "And if you think they're all after you now – you just wait until they see the cover of the next issue of *Horsing Around*! She raised her hands in the air as if she were spelling out a headline. "Seventeen-year-old newcomer makes dream ride to win at Kentucky!"

She smiled at Issie. "This is a total scoop. I'm giving the story at least ten pages. Just wait until my readers discover the truth behind the scenes too – all about Valmont and the sinister goings-on at his stables. My dear, you are the biggest news to hit the eventing world in years," Tiggy insisted. "And you've still got the Grand Slam to come."

"The Grand Slam?" Issie said.

"You've just won Kentucky, dear," Tiggy said. "You're going for the Grand Slam, aren't you?"

The Grand Slam was the holy grail for eventing riders, the most famous prize of all. To win the Grand Slam, a rider had to win three of the world's most famous Four-Star events all in the space of one year. The first of these events was the Kentucky Four-Star, and the other two were both based in the UK. There were the Burghley Horse Trials – a few months away, and the Badminton Horse Trials, in just two weeks' time!

"Of course Issie's going for the Grand Slam!" Avery said, answering Tiggy's question. "It's always been Issie's intention to ride at Badminton and Burghley this season. Her entry has been accepted for both events. Two of her best horses have qualified and the paperwork has been completed."

Tiggy was frantically taking notes, her eyes bright with excitement at this latest twist. "But can you do it?" she asked Issie. "Badminton Horse Trials are in a fortnight. There's no way you can get Comet back to the UK from the USA in time."

"I'm not riding Comet," Issie said. "I've got another horse at Laurel Farm."

"Another horse?" Tiggy was intrigued.

"Uh-huh. I was saving him for Badminton – but we were really strapped for cash and I thought I might have to sell him."

"Well, you're not poor any more, dear," Tiggy told her. "Like I just said, you'll have sponsorship dosh coming out of your ears."

Today was getting more and more incredible. Issie

wouldn't need to sell Nightstorm after all. Instead, she would be riding him at the Badminton Horse Trials!

When Issie began riding lessons at pony club she had always dreamt that one day she would ride in a real Four-Star competition – and today that dream had become reality in the most incredible way. But already her thoughts were turning to Badminton and Burghley. The two competitions were considered to be the very pinnacle of the sport. They were the most challenging, dangerous and thrilling horse trials in the whole world. And Issie was going to be competing in them. More than that, she had to be ready for Badminton in just two weeks' time!

But right now Issie could hear Mike Partridge's voice calling her back into the stadium. The dignitaries and officials had gathered for the awards presentation and a hush had fallen over the crowd.

Issie rode back into the centre of the arena on the silver-dapple mare who was now an eventing sensation. Liberty seemed to know that she was the star as she stood perfectly still for the judges to tie the red satin winner's sash round her, and the head of the Equestrian Federation trod across the arena in her high heels to place a floral wreath of snow-white roses carefully round the mare's neck. And then, to the cheers of the crowd and the sound of a trumpet fanfare, Issie took Liberty on her victory lap, waving to crowds and to the cameras that were beaming the images around the world.

In New Zealand, her friends and family watched the victory lap and cheered on a local hero. Meanwhile, on the other side of the world, in a farm kitchen in the heart of Wiltshire, Francoise D'Arth watched the very same ceremony on Laurel Farm's tiny TV set. There were tears in her eyes as she watched Issie take off her helmet and wave to the crowds. She stayed glued to the screen until the ceremony was over, and then she went back out to the stables. The horses stuck their heads over the loose-box doors to greet Francoise, just as they always did, hoping that it might be dinnertime.

They were all beautiful and talented eventers, but there was one horse in particular that stood out from the rest, and it was this horse, the athletic bay stallion with the white blaze that the French trainer had come to see with her news.

"She's done it," Francoise whispered to the big bay. "She's won Kentucky."

In his stall, Nightstorm nickered and shifted restlessly, as if he understood what this meant – for the girl and for him. The win in Kentucky was just the beginning. Issie Brown was coming back to the UK to be reunited with her beloved stallion and together they would face up to the greatest eventing challenge, the competitions of Badminton and Burghley – and the dream of the Grand Slam.

STACY GREGG

PONY  CLUB SECRETS

Nightstorm and the Grand Slam

Issie Brown's dreams are coming true as she competes on the British Four-Star eventing circuit. Can she and beloved sporthorse, Nightstorm, triumph against the world's best riders at Badminton and Burghley?

HarperCollins *Children's Books*

STACY GREGG

PONY CLUB SECRETS

Book One

Mystic and the Midnight Ride

Issie LOVES horses and is a member of the Chevalier Point Pony Club, where she looks after her pony Mystic, trains for gymkhanas and hangs out with her best friends.

When Issie is asked to train Blaze, an abandoned pony, her riding skills are put to the test. Can she tame the spirited new horse? And is Blaze really out of danger?

HarperCollins *Children's Books*

STACY GREGG

PONY CLUB SECRETS

Book Two

Blaze and the Dark Rider

Issie and her friends have been picked to represent the
Chevalier Point Pony Club at the Interclub Shield – the
biggest competition of the year. It's time to get training!

But when equipment is sabotaged and one of the riders
is injured, Issie and her friends are determined to find
out who's to blame...

HarperCollins *Children's Books*

Saddle up for the PONY CLUB RIVALS series

also by Stacy Gregg:

Coming soon:

www.stacygregg.co.uk